Charm City

THE DEMON WHISPERER #1

ASH KRAFTON

Red Fist Fiction

Cover art: Red Fist Fiction
Interior design/formatting: Red Fist Fiction

First edition published 2016

Contact Information can be found at **www.ashkrafton.com**

Charm City (The Demon Whisperer #1) by Ash Krafton

The darkness is rising and one man stands against it: the exorcist mage Simon Alliant. But in Baltimore, he finally meets his match...a part-mortal divinity with the power to whisper away demons.

ISBN-10: 1-946120-03-0
ISBN-13: 978-1-946120-03-8

Charm City:
The Demon Whisperer
Book One

by Ash Krafton

DEDICATION

For my husband, my children, my family:
apologies for putting the *ick* in magic
(and by "apologies" I really mean
"sorry I'm not sorry")

ACKNOWLEGMENT

Special thanks to everyone at Wattpad.com—the writers who encouraged me to join up, the staff who selected CHARM CITY to be a Featured Story, and every single reader who found their way into this book.

Extra special thanks to the readers who commented their way through the story, giving me a play-by-play. I can't tell you how much fun it is to watch someone read and react to a story I wrote. More than makes up for tons of hours spent tapping keys in an empty room. To ruin a line by the Bard himself: *What books are books if readers be not by?*

I've never met a more enthusiastic and interesting group of readers and writers and I am so honored to be a part of this creative collective. Keep reading, keep writing, and keep sharing words with the world because words are our gift, our foundation, our way to connect with one another.

Cheers and happy reading,
Ash

TABLE OF CONTENTS

PROLOGUE..13
CHAPTER 1...17
CHAPTER 2...23
CHAPTER 3...32
CHAPTER 4...39
CHAPTER 5...50
CHAPTER 6...60
CHAPTER 7...69
CHAPTER 8...76
CHAPTER 9...83
CHAPTER 10...91
CHAPTER 11.......................................108
CHAPTER 12.......................................117
CHAPTER 13.......................................125
CHAPTER 14.......................................136
CHAPTER 15.......................................147
CHAPTER 16.......................................153
CHAPTER 17.......................................158
CHAPTER 18.......................................166
CHAPTER 19.......................................173
CHAPTER 20.......................................183
CHAPTER 21.......................................189
EPILOGUE..197
ABOUT THE AUTHOR.........................203

"Who is more foolish, the child afraid of the dark
or the man afraid of the light?"

~Maurice Freehill (1899-1939)

three years ago
Saint Berenice's Rehabilitation Center
near Boston, Massachusetts

Boston (AP) - Police may have uncovered new evidence in a cold case that has baffled authorities for the past fifteen years.

Ten-year-old Sarah Foster disappeared from her home in Belmont in 1998, the same night the body of a local teen had been discovered in a nearby playground. Although no connection between the two victims had ever been found, authorities believe they may have uncovered a link that may lead them to finally solve these cases.

Evidence has recently been recovered from the belongings of a former patient of the Green Field Care Facility, in Malden.

Workers at Green Field claim that Norma Alliant, who passed away last week, had become lucid in the hours leading up her passing. Day shift nurse manager Janna Thomas said she didn't pay attention at first, since Alliant was known for frequent vocalizations. But when Alliant mentioned the name of the girl who'd disappeared, Thomas said she took notice.

"She talked about that little girl as if she knew her," Thomas

said. "I know it was a long time ago, but we all grew up with the stories. We all feel like we know her somehow. And we all knew the horror stories about how Ritchie Evans was killed. But then she got agitated, screaming about Sarah and that boy that was killed at the park and she started scratching herself."

Thomas said Alliant passed peacefully later that same evening.

The detective was contacted shortly after the autopsy, when the coroner noticed the self-inflicted scratch marks bore a striking similarity to mysterious symbols that had been associated with the Evans case. The coroner recognized them because he had been the same doctor to examine the victim's remains.

"These symbols were evidence that had never been made public," said Corcoran. "We have reason to believe that there may be others who have information regarding these unsolved cases."

Alliant had no local family. The whereabouts of her next of kin are currently being investigated.

Members of neither the Foster nor the Evans families could be reached for comment.

Police urge citizens to contact officials if they recall anything about either of these cases or if they recognize these strange symbols.

"In other news…" The news anchorwoman switched topics without blinking, as if the report were just another day in the life. To her, it was.

It just wasn't her life. No worries.

Simon Alliant stared at the screen, his brain a blank buzz. Sitting on the edge of the metal hospital bed, he cracked his neck and rolled his shoulders, grimacing. A heavy moment dragged by.

The buzz snapped off. The rage took over.

He snatched up the remote and switched off the TV, then threw the remote at it, then dragged the set down off the rack. The television crashed onto the floor, sparks and shards flying in all directions. Dark eyes lit by a mad gleam, he searched the starkly-furnished white room, looking for something else to destroy, something else to ruin.

Something other than himself, for once. Just this god-dammed once.

Panting, he sank to his knees, heels of his palms pressed into his eyes. Defeated. Teeth gritted, he groaned, a sound of deep pain. Always, defeated. No matter how hard he fought, no matter what price he paid, he always ended up here, on his knees, begging for help from the one source he should never, ever, not ever again seek.

Sullenly, he rolled up his sleeve. Maybe, just once. One more time and that will be it. He'll come out on top. A tattoo of a circular-shaped rune, the size of a quarter, stained the inside bend of his elbow, directly over the vein. He rubbed it, eyes unfocused, his frown deepening. The only one he ever could lie to was himself. And this was the only time he believed those lies.

Times like this, lies were the only comfort he had.

Grimacing, he took a slender object out of the pocket of his thin cotton robe. He pulled the cap off with his teeth and spit it out. Muttering under his breath, he positioned the object over the tattoo and squeezed his eyes shut.

The words made little sense, even to him, but they were perfect, precise, articulate, growing louder and harder with each repetition of the verse. When his voice reached a frenzied pitch he jabbed the object downward into his arm, into the tattoo.

The tattoo glowed.

A streak of orange zipped around the outermost ring of ink with a metallic sizzle. Eyes flew open wide, pinpoint pupils making tiny splots against irises of pale gray. He sucked air in through his teeth and he let out a ragged cry before going limp, sagging to the floor, eyes half-closed. The object rolled out of his slackened fingers.

It wasn't a needle. It was a thin wooden dowel, stained and carved and worn smooth by too much handling. It was a wand.

Not all addictions were chemical.

He blinked once, then again, his vision blurring, his hearing muffled by the pounding of blood in his ears. He barely registered the clank of the lock sliding open, or the door flung open against the wall, or the frantic voice of the orderly who rushed in.

The attendant slapped roughly at his cheeks, trying to revive him. The weary smile on Simon's face never faded, not even as he passed out and the world faded away, stranding him in boneless, blissful oblivion.

"You seem much improved, Mr. Murphy." The social worker folded her hands on top of his file, a fat many-paged collection of his previous ins and outs. Saint Berenice had become more than a temporary lay-over. It was starting to feel like home.

Which meant he'd stayed too long. "Feeling better, sweetheart. Time I move on."

"But you were extremely vulnerable when you arrived. I must insist." She shook her head, peering into his eyes.

He avoided that burrowing gaze and stared at the folder. A photograph was paper-clipped to the cover, the name KEVIN MURPHY printed in block letters across the top. Dark hair, dark eyes. What his mom would have called "properly Black Irish", clipped and shaved like a dandy. He snorted a soft derisive sound, knowing that he looked nothing like that when he was at his worst. That's the picture they should have—rumpled shirt, straggly almost-beard, dark rings beneath gray ghost eyes, the magic still burning through his veins. *On the wagon* was such a school boy look.

"Kevin." Her voice made him look up again. "For your

own sake."

"I'm not doing this for my sake. I'm doing it for yours."

She bit her lips, a look of resignation on her face. "I think that this is premature. You feel rested, don't you? You look healthier. But it wasn't just anxiety that brought you back here, or the worry of a relapse. You are avoiding the true reason you haven't attained peace."

"I avoid a lot of stuff. It's how I stay alive."

"But your addiction—"

"You don't know the first thing about my addiction." Simon regretted the sharpness of his tone but was unable to soften it. "Don't presume the answer lies here among your group therapy and your Jungian theories and your psychological voodoo. If I say I'm better, it's because it's as better as I'm going to get."

A long silence passed between them. She'd never been anything but polite to him, even helpful at times; the game was different now. Truths were going to out themselves, truths that tended to drag everyone nearby down with them. He'd hurt her, just now. He couldn't prevent collateral damage but he had a duty to minimize it. Even if it meant he had to be an asshole to do it.

"You have to sign here to discharge yourself against doctor's orders," she said, her voice heavy. She flipped open the back cover to a printed medical form.

"I checked myself in." He took her pen and signed the bottom of the paper with a flourish. *Kevin Murphy.* As good a name as any, but he could never get the letter *v* right. Maybe it was time for a new alias. "I can do the same in reverse."

The therapist sighed and closed the file. She pulled a yellow envelope out of a basket. Opening it, she tipped the contents out onto the signed paperwork.

Wallet, cell phone, wristwatch, religious medallions, the

wand. It rolled toward him and he snatched it up, shoving it into his breast pocket before collecting the other items. "Ah. My worry-stick. I was looking for that."

"Kevin, I don't think a simple worry-stick is enough to conquer the demons inside you."

"We'll not talk about my demons, sweetheart. Not when they can hear you." His smile faded, his eyes going glassy and hard. "Until next time, eh?"

He snapped an about-face and strode out of her office, down the taupe-colored hallway toward the door, pausing until he heard the electronic buzz of the lock release. He left the facility, doors slamming shut behind him.

The air was balmy, remnants of sea air tainted by traffic fumes as it filtered through miles of city sprawl. Ah. He inhaled deeply through his nose. The smell of freedom. Good to be out and about again.

Then again, he'd had a similar thought when he checked himself in month ago. Shrugging, he straightened his jacket and set off toward the news stand on the corner. Freedom came in many forms.

He hadn't made it to the sidewalk before a warm wind and the scent of clean linen surrounded him.

"Simon."

He caught the whispered sound of his real name and tilted his head toward it.

His real name was nearly an unknown thing these days, especially after having played the role of Kevin Murphy, career mental case and junkie from Boston's darker side. He'd created the alias so long ago that he'd nearly forgotten the details of Kevin's manufactured life.

If only his time as Kevin allowed him to forget his life as Simon.

Looking around, he spotted a tall, pale man wearing a tunic and loose pants, leaning against a tree. Sandy brown hair fell in soft curls to his shoulders, framing a sculpted face that seemed unbeguiling.

So out of place in modern Boston. If the dude wasn't careful, he'd get mugged. Good thing he was more or less invisible to ordinary people.

The tall man straightened himself and walked toward him. A vague mist hung about his shoulders, trailing behind him like a shadowy fog.

It would have seemed unnatural if Simon didn't spend so much time hanging about on the wrong side of nature. Odd mists weren't enough to put him off. They weren't even enough for him to mention.

"Mack." Simon looked him up and down. Sandals. Another reason to mug him. He really needed to get with the times. "Long time, no see. What, you couldn't visit even once? Not even on Tuesdays? We had Taco Tuesdays, buddy. You really missed out."

"You were trying to regain your sanity, Simon." The man's voice was smooth and melodious, a mild accent that couldn't be pinned down to any one region. Or millennium, for that matter. "I doubt visions of an angel would have helped."

"Shoot, sanity. It was good old R and R."

"Was it, now?" Mack pursed his lips, eyebrows raised. He had a very human-like quality to his features, if one ignored the ghost of his wings. "I thought it was…antidepressants and group therapy."

"Well, the first week or two. But then nothing but spa days from there on out."

"Mmm." The angel smiled, a gentle radiance that elevated his already-beautiful features. "A solid month of being magic-free? How did it feel?"

Simon ruffled his hair. He couldn't lie, not to the one entity that had never lied to him. *Magic* and *free* never belonged in the same sentence. "Feels like I can use a smoke. Shall I buy my ciggies now or after we land?"

"After. We need to get your boots on the ground right away."

"I just got out of the looney bin, pal. Give me a moment to acclimate."

Mack slowly shook his head. "There was a gathering at the Ladder today. Simon…the darkness is rising."

"Why not?" Simon hung his head, defeated. "Can we just skip the Metatron light show and just have the down and dirty? They held my afternoon Valium and my head is splitting."

"But you lose the surety—"

"I've never gotten anything but the straight shit from you, Mack. So let's have it."

"There is a…traitor."

He rolled his eyes. Half of Mack's heavenly announcements began with those same words. "There's always a traitor. Why does this one get divine attention?"

"Because it's an internal concern. A child of the Light has one foot in the darkness. It needs to be handled…delicately."

"And you need good old Simon Alliant to be the heavy. Figures. Nobody else willing to get their wings dirty." He cracked his neck and spared a forlorn glance at the newsstand down the street. "Where, this time?"

"Baltimore."

Simon groaned. The original Charm City. He'd taken a great deal of ribbing from an old master about previous sojourns there. A man who used amulets for a living had no business in a city with so trite a nickname. "I hate being that close to D.C."

"You can complain afterwards." The angel stepped behind Simon and wrapped his arms around his chest, emitting a soft glow that began to encompass them both.

"I usually do." Simon closed his eyes, waiting for the pull and the drop.

The power hit swiftly like freefall, pulling his breath out in a gush.

For a moment, his essence was caught between two places, his molecules stretched apart, his spirit suspended in a void. Memory couldn't reach him here. His past couldn't catch up to him here. It was a perfect singularity, this being in the now.

True freedom, the shortest lived of its kind. Yet the perfection of the moment was tainted. Tainted with a dread he couldn't outrun.

He dreaded the inevitable instant this tiny reprieve would end.

current day
The Devil's Drink
Baltimore, Maryland

Simon Alliant hated nightclubs.

Tourist trap clubs, anyway, with their aseptic furniture and the plastic and chrome and high ceilings and LED lights. They were poor competition to the places he'd frequented in his youth—dingy basement bars with small stages that barely fit a five-man band, people packed up against the edge like kettle fish. When the music started and the lights glared, the crowd bounced like a single, mindless mass.

The humanity, the press of flesh, the scents of smoke and skin and sweat. The often-predictable drunken fist fight and resulting overnight stay in the city can.

He smiled a little, reminiscing. Ah. The good old days.

But not here. Who came up with the name for this place, anyway? The Devil's Drink? Hardly. He spared a glance at the neon-lit walls and white plastic stools. Places like this always felt more like after hours in a hospital when the med cabinet was left unlocked. Potential for a good time, but not quite making it.

This one was definitely too clean for his taste. Everything was blue and silver, a desperate attempt to capture an ethereal feel. It might have succeeded, if one were drunk enough and crossed his eyes. But not tonight.

Tonight, he was on the clock.

He weaved his way through the *haute couture* and the slick-styled posh. Mostly new university graduates living far beyond their means. None of these kids earned enough to wear the clothes or drive the cars they did, unless they'd made some sort of deal with the devil.

And, as far as he knew, there was only bloke here who'd actually done just that.

The bar looked like a chemistry laboratory. More of that aseptic feel, futuristic glass and colorful decanters, minus the white laboratory coats. It didn't feel like a place to slake a thirst or drown a sorrow.

"Hey." He lifted his chin at the bartender to get his attention. And failed. The bartender passed him by three times without pausing or even making eye contact.

Grumbling, Simon pulled a ten-dollar bill out of his pocket and smoothed it out, folding it sharply lengthwise, before holding it like a flag between two fingers. This time, he didn't even need to make eye contact with the kid, who manifested in front of him within seconds.

Of course. Money worked its own magic.

"What will it be?"

"Martini, squeaky clean. Oh, and hold the vermouth."

The bartender rolled his eyes before reaching under the bar for the cheap gin.

Thirty seconds later, Simon was staring at an oddly misshapen twist of glassware. Looking down the length of the bar, he noticed others drinking from similar vessels.

What the hell am I supposed to do with this? I can't even figure out how to drink out of this fricken thing.

Finally, he admitted defeat. He signaled to the bartender. "Can I get a glass?"

With a sour look, the bartender reached under the bar. He popped a plain tumbler in front of him. "Would you like a straw?"

Simon grinned and nodded. "Good one."

He examined the garnish briefly before determining it was inedible, and tossed it onto the napkin before sloshing the gin into the glass.

Seeing the bartender's disdain, he raised the glass in a mock toast. "Cheers."

He raised the glass to his lips and paused. It wasn't the acrid pineyness of the booze that stopped him from drinking. A spike of metaphysical energy hit him like the bite of a bad grounding.

The edges of his senses tingled, a prickling deep in his brain. He didn't even have to try to notice it. This was a part of himself that never shut off. It was always watchful, waiting.

His gaze jerked to the side and he cocked his head before grimacing, his face awash in a cold humor.

"All work and no play." Shaking his head, he clunked the glass down with a rueful smile. "Alright, pal. Let's have a look at you."

With a kick against the bar, he slowly spun his barstool around. He slipped a lens out of his pocket and held it up in front of his eye and scanned the crowd.

Through the scrying lens, the light scattered into rainbow streaks. Kind of like an infrared camera, except this didn't detect heat—it detected divine energy. Particularly, hell stain. Came in real handy when looking for the bad guys.

As he surveyed the room, he noticed a figure near the wall, so much different than all the others. That figure glowed a dark, seething red, dripping heat.

He lowered the lens to see an otherwise normal-looking guy, talking up a pretty brunette.

Simon stowed the lens in his jacket pocket. "Righto, then. Time to crash his little party."

He picked up his drink, centered himself, then wove his way through the crowd with a tipsy smile. Despite his cheerful blunders when he artfully bumped into this one and that, he never took his eyes off the guy.

The guy leaned over the woman, his hand on the wall behind her. She played with the straw in her drink, obviously enthralled with him. Such intense conversation. How can they hear each other over the racket? And, he knew, she shouldn't want to hear him. Not if she had any idea what he was, or what his words could do.

She raised up on her toes to whisper in his ear and slipped her hand around his neck. Over her shoulder, the kid's eyes flashed a sinister red glow.

God help her. She didn't realize she was hooking up with a demon.

No time to waste. Hell wasn't going to ruin another innocent girl. Not while he was still able to do something about it.

He shot through the crowd like an arrow, slowing his last steps to an exaggerated stagger. Tripping over his feet, he wedged himself between the couple.

"Ah, thought I smelled a party." He grinned and looped an arm around each of their necks. "Mind if I join?"

With a huff, the woman flipped his arm off and pushed him back. Her touch was surprisingly gentle, considering the expression on her face. Her eyebrows were practically touching, though, she was so put out. "Why don't you get lost, buddy?"

Simon swung his face close to hers, his voice low and steely. "You're the one who needs to skedaddle. I got business with my friend here."

She pinched her lips, then took a deep breath. "He's not your friend."

"And he really shouldn't be yours." Reaching into his side pocket, he pulled out a bundle of woven reeds, the center darkened by a metal charm that had been seared into it. St. Bridget's cross, with a touch of St. Michael for good measure.

A measure well taken. The demon screamed at the sight of it and recoiled, temporarily losing control on its human guise. Its mouth stretched impossibly wide, teeth like wicked needles, eyes ablaze with red fury.

Simon smiled a mean slant. Watching a demon writhe in agony did wonders for a guy's spirits.

For as long as it lasted, anyway, which wasn't more than a few moments. Before he could utter the binding spell, the demon-possessed man broke and ran, deftly snaking through the crowd toward the exit.

The woman looked stunned. Apparently she wasn't accustomed to being ditched. Poor girl. The first taste of disappointment was always a bitter one.

"Well, can't say I didn't try." Simon stowed the cross, unwilling to waste any of its considerable power on the trivialities of the passing immoral. "No need to thank me, love."

"Damn straight there isn't. I should throttle you." She glared at him a moment before pushing past him, sending him against the wall with a surprising amount of force.

He stared after her, his jaw slacking. She was going after the bastard.

"What in hell...?" He shook his head before scrambling

to catch up. Some girls just couldn't take no for an answer.

The streets were damp and noisy, car traffic in an endless stream in front of the popular club. Simon ignored the pedestrians, the line of people waiting to get in. Rounding the corner, he scanned the alley before stepping out of the safety of the streetlights into the shadows beyond. He extended his hands out, as if walking in the dark. Not that he worried about bumping into a wall or a dumpster—it was the spiritual dark he feared. Eyes half-closed, he let the sensitive part of his brain go wide open. Taking a stiff inhale, he lifted his chin.

A trace of rancid smoke wound its way like a ribbon through the heavy air. The demon's wake.

He followed the trail, deeper into the alley, the smell growing stronger. There, in a recessed doorway, he spied the couple in an embrace.

The woman's back was to Simon, the only visible part of the demon his arms wrapped around her. Below the rolled-up sleeves and weight-room biceps, the flesh was marred, molten and gnarled, ending in hands that were blackened, scaled, and claw-tipped.

Its face was hidden in the shadows. Over the woman's shoulder gleamed twin slits of baleful red.

"Shit." Simon muttered as he assessed the demon's appearance. The human host was disappearing, little by little. Only a matter of time before it took full control. "Hey! You there!"

The demon snarled. *GO AWAY.* A myriad of voices twisted the syllables into an unholy chorus.

"Ugh." The woman half-turned to glance at Simon. "You again? Can't you see I'm busy?

"Sure, you are." He popped thick matching rings onto his thumbs and spread his hands apart, stretching a glowing hum between his palms, collecting power that zapped and sparked around the odd silver circles. The light quickly built to an opaque glow.

"In the name of the Light, I draw thee." His gaze firmly on the demon's eyes, Simon chanted the binding spell. "In the name of the Light, I bind thee. In the name of the Light, I cast thee back into darkness. In the name of the Light, I—"

The demon screamed in loathsome rage, the collection of voices reaching an ear-splitting pitch, but it could not look away from the exorcist who held it in thrall. It pushed the woman aside and stumbled forward, writhing in pain.

Suddenly, the host hunched over, crunching tight against his knees, dropping to the ground. Tighter, tighter he folded himself, impossibly smaller, shrinking down until he imploded.

The demon planed out and disappeared, taking the host with it. The power snap impacted Simon so hard he had to take a step back to brace himself. A very human scream echoed off the walls of the buildings, reverberating into the distance.

"No, no, no, no!" Simon bit back a curse and rubbed a hand over the back of his head, ruffling his hair as he tried to massage away the ache in his brain. "That should have worked."

He lifted his hands like antennae, hoping to catch the tail-end of the demon's wake. There was nothing. Not a damn thing. "Sorry 'bout that, sweetheart. Go on back to your clubbing. And for the love of all that's decent, stay away from that one."

The woman stared at him, utterly agape. Probably not used to guys being all hands one minute and imploding into brimstone smoke the next. Well, she was still alive. She'd get over it.

Or not.

She rushed him and stuck with both hands flat on his chest, knocking him back a pace. "What are you doing?"

"Protecting you from a certain end, that's what."

"He was listening to me." She looked mad enough to spit. "I just about had him!"

"You shouldn't have needed a second warning and you definitely shouldn't have gotten a second chance." He nosed into her, genuine steel in his eyes. "You just remember, sweetheart. Third time is always the charm—and you don't have the right charm to survive."

For a moment, she looked like she wanted to hit him, hard.

He merely turned aside and lit a cigarette. It wasn't merely a matter of dismissing her—turning his hips would protect his assets, the most likely target of a woman scorned.

She put her hands up in a "whatever" gesture and left with a huff. Halfway to the sidewalk, she turned to yell over her shoulder. "Don't mess with things you don't understand."

Of all the things—he just saved her sweet behind from a demon. A *demon*. Not some tanked-up pretty-boy college kid who had drunk himself past the God's-Gift-To-Woman stage and halfway to Bulletproof. A demon, with enough power to completely transform a mortal body. According to the rules of divinity and mortality, it shouldn't have been able to do that, not out in the open like that.

Obviously, she didn't know what a demon like that could do to a waify little something like her. He expected better manners. It was getting tiresome, this business of having his expectations fall flat, time and time again.

At the full end of his patience, he decided if she didn't

need manners, neither did he. "Yeah, well," he called after her. "Maybe you haven't heard of me. Demons are my business."

At the word *demon*, she stopped in her tracks.

That got her attention, now, didn't it? He dragged deep on his cigarette, chuffing out the smoke in disgust.

She issued an irritated huff and spun around, stomping back over to him. Grabbing his hand, she looked hard at his face, pressing closer, until they were nearly nose to nose.

Her touch disoriented him, numbing the special part of his brain. A murmuring of jumbled voices filled his head. A shuffling sensation, a trip, a fall, a drop that he felt in his stomach—

It cut off when she dropped his hand with a snort.

"Well, I've heard of you now, Simon Alliant." She turned to leave again, rolling her eyes. "Exorcist and demonologist, indeed. You're just a fool bumbling through life with a fistful of charms."

Simon opened his mouth to speak but all semblance of coherent language had deserted him. All except for one word: gob-smacked. Trying to scoop his senses back together, he shook off the last of the confusion.

"Now, wait a minute." He smiled, open-mouthed, and waved a finger in her general direction. "I'm the only one who gets to say that."

She turned the corner, out of sight. He followed after her at a run but, by the time he reached the street, she was gone.

Leaning against the front of a convenience store, Simon slid out his last cigarette and crumpled the empty pack. Nothing. Two days of constant vigilance and nothing to show for it. The demon hadn't left enough of a trace for him to identify it, let alone bind it. When it planed out, it planed out completely.

He rubbed his eyes, but his vision wouldn't clear. Everywhere he looked, he saw a thin trace of demonic energy, like a layer of muddy watercolor. Just nothing specific. He revisited the last manifestation site, retracing his steps. Nothing in the club. Nothing in the alley. No leads on the identity of the host kid.

No sign of that girl.

It was a relentless search, fueled by cheap coffee, cigarettes, fast food. He'd pause for a quick nod-off in a diner bathroom stall before hitting the streets again. If only this headache would quit—maybe a pair of sunglasses would dim that damned useless shadow he saw everywhere.

Exhaling a plume of pale smoke, he flicked the butt into the parking lot before ducking into the convenience store. Coffee at this shop was consistently terrible, either too strong or piteously weak depending on who was working.

Eying the clerk and the long line waiting at the counter, he grimaced. Weak brew it was, then. Extra cream couldn't fix that.

He poured a large cup, no cream, and dropped in two caffeine tablets—the working man's answer to sugar. At least the bitter taste would help mask the lack of actual coffee flavor. While waiting in line, he paged through a newspaper. No leads there, either—not a single mention of an odd occurrence or unexplainable accident. That was the trouble with mainstream journalism—nobody ever reported the paranormal junk. How easy would that make his life?

Once back outside, he squinted into the sunlight, slapping a new pack of Marlboros against the palm of his hand, wondering which direction to take.

He smelled it first, an acrid stench like burning plastic. Always had a knack for standing downwind of demons. Lucky, that.

Turning his head, he spied the guy sitting on the bus-stop bench at the corner. The host's spine was ram-rod stiff, his neck bent at an uncomfortable angle. The demon had been inside him for so long that he'd forgotten how to position his body.

Simon exhaled a whisper, the words of a protective spell, while thumbing the ring on his middle finger, twisting it in a complete circle. Carved from galena taken from an abandoned mine in Sardinia, the silver charm was purported to hide one's magical signature, rendering the wearer invisible to magical sight.

Maybe it worked. He couldn't be sure. Most of the time, he twisted it out of a nervous tick. He approached slowly, holding his breath, not relying solely on the charm to keep him from being detected. Step by step, just behind the normal range of peripheral vision, he moved closer.

The guy stared straight ahead, head jerking, with irregular twitches. A thin line of drool seeped out of his mouth, his lips twisted in a snarl. He muttered like a dog having an angry dream.

Another spot of movement drew Simon's attention. There was a person on the bench next to the kid.

Simon's insides curdled. Damn it. A bystander. A complication he didn't want. He rubbed his mouth, watching, hoping the problem would fix itself. Maybe the bus would come around the corner. Maybe they'd start to wonder about the weirdo sitting next to them. Common sense wasn't completely extinct, right?

The person leaned forward into view, her face tilted up toward the host's.

And damn it again. He rolled his lips between his teeth. It was her. Again. This girl was ridiculous.

She un-crossed her legs and scooted closer to him, her lips moving. Talking. She was talking to him. Talking, as if he wasn't ready to explode in a rain of hell fire, perhaps quite literally.

Arms crossed, Simon intentionally side-stepped into her line of sight. She didn't break her gaze with the host, who had started shuddering like a malfunctioning robot.

"Stay back, Simon." She raised her voice only enough to carry, her tone sing-songy and soothing. "He's listening."

"And he's getting ready to blow." He flexed his fingers, fisting and releasing in tense anticipation. "Let me take care of this."

"Don't be a fool," she said. "It would be really poor judgment on your part."

She reached up toward the demon's face, whispering.

Suddenly, the guy relaxed, going limp, like a marionette

whose strings had just been cut. His head fell back, mouth slack, eyes rolled. A stream of thin black smoke rushed out of his mouth with a sizzle. The smoke, scented like rotten eggs, flitted past Simon before dissipating on a steady breeze.

Slowly, the guy pulled himself upright, glancing warily around in apparent confusion.

Simon took a swig of coffee and grimaced. Small wonder. He hadn't really been himself for days.

"Where am I?" The man rubbed his face with both hands and tried to stand. His legs weren't ready to hold him. He dropped back down on the bench with a thump.

"Baltimore." The woman patted his leg. "You're okay, now. You were possessed."

"Oh, right. I bet." His grogginess faded, replaced with a cockiness that dripped from every word. "By a demon, right?"

"Yes, by a demon." She dipped her head in a nod. "There is no other kind of possession." She tugged a silver tin out of her purse and opened it. Sunlight glinted wetly off its contents. She dipped her finger into it, scooping up a glob of clear sparkly jelly. Whispering, she traced the shape of a cross on his forehead.

"You opened yourself up to darkness," she said, and snapped the tin shut with a *snick*. "Don't want it to happen again? Keep your thoughts and your intentions in the light. Make good choices. It's the only way to keep the darkness from taking you again."

She stowed the tin before getting up and walking away, sparing only a glance at Simon as she passed him.

"Hang on." Simon pivoted and locked step with her. "You exorcised that demon."

"And I could have done it days ago if you would have minded your own business."

They both paused to look back at the man, who had raised hesitant fingers to the smear on his forehead.

The woman cleared her throat. "I wouldn't wipe that off if I were you."

Looking shaken, the guy found his feet and loped off, casting distressed glances over his shoulder until he rounded the corner.

"I've never seen a soft exorcism before," Simon said. "How did you do that?"

Tucking a strand of hair behind her ear, she looked up at him. "I convinced the entity it was his own idea."

He chuffed out a laugh. "So you sweet-talk a demon out of a possession. Who are you?"

She eyed him for a long moment before answering. "Chiara," she replied, a bit hesitant. "And I'm leaving."

"Not alone, you're not."

She paused and leveled a look at him. Something about the eyes. A bit too shiny, as if they had their own source of illumination. He remembered the way she'd rifled through his mind when she grabbed him the other night. Obviously, this was no ordinary girl.

Best to stay out of arm's reach, anyhow. No telling what else this demon whisperer could do.

A tiny voice in his head insisted the safest thing to do would be to put as much distance between them as possible. It was overruled by the majority, the part that thirsted for knowledge and the undiscovered. Running away wasn't an option. Self-preservation always came in second to his curiosity.

And the curiosity was chewing at him. "Come on," he said. "I just want to talk. Those were some pretty sick moves. I've got a billion questions."

"Questions that are better left unanswered." Her tone was firm.

It sounded like she was putting up a tough front, but her body language said something different. She twisted the strap of her purse, looking undecided.

Undecided was something he could work with. "Commiseration, then. Celebrate the victory of another successful cleansing. How often do exorcists get together without trying to kill each other?"

"I get the feeling if I remain around you too long, I *will* try." The corners of her mouth twitched toward a possible grin.

"Well, then. We must be destined for greatness, since only my closest friends feel like that."

"I shouldn't. I work alone. I've always worked alone."

"But we're on the same side. Allies, right? What's wrong with allies sharing information if it furthers the cause?" He tried to look innocent and harmless and knew it would never look genuine. "Not talking about moving in. Just talk."

"All right." She sighed, looking defeated but not wretchedly disappointed. Good sign. "At least make yourself useful and buy me a drink. I'm exhausted."

He grinned. She exorcised demons, she was good for a snappy comeback, and she liked a drink before noon. What else would they have in common? "I think I like you."

"Yeah, well." She shook her head and hoisted her purse onto her other shoulder. "There's your poor judgment again. One day, it will land you in serious trouble."

"Eh. Trouble's my middle name."

"And you think that's a good thing?"

"I'm still alive, ain't I?"

"Don't take it for granted." She poked him in the chest. "That's subject to change at any given moment."

"Yeah." He shoved his hands into his pocket, toying

with the jangle of charms. He knew each one by touch, by the tiny zing of power each one played against his fingertips. Didn't have to see them. He could find them in the dark. And sometimes…the dark was bigger than he was. "Tell me about it."

"I would, but I get the feeling you already know." She pivoted on her heel and walked away. "Just—forget it."

"Wait. Please." How else could he convince her? He dug deep, deeper than he had for anyone in a long time. Past the flippant remarks that coated his mouth, always the first words out. Past the charms jingling in his pocket. Past the impulse to use magic, to force the outcome, to turn the situation to his liking.

He knew none of that would work with her. He reached past all of it to his deepest core, where the eternal apprentice dwelled. "It is foolish to guard against misfortunes from the external world and leave the inner mind uncontrolled."

She stopped in her tracks.

"Just talk," he called. "That's all."

This time, when she turned to look at him, there was no slick gleam in her eyes.

Simon pulled open the door of the bar and gestured to Chiara to go in. He paused behind her in the doorway, taking a deep, appreciative breath.

Now this—this was a bar. If the word "seedy" wasn't the first to come to mind when he walked in the door, it probably wasn't his kind of place. And this one definitely was his kind of place.

Dim lighting, most of it through the greasy windows. He took a deep inhale through his nose. Stale smoke, fryers in the kitchen with oil just this side of gone bad. Old jukebox that hadn't been updated since the early nineties, which was fine by him. Handful of solitary patrons, mostly third shifters getting ready to call it a night.

He pointed out two seats in the front corner and followed her around the bend of the dinged-up U-shaped bar. He liked to be able to see the front door, and he didn't like foot traffic behind him. Regular bartender wasn't the chatty kind but he was clean and seemed to be trying to make an honest living. Bobby had a simple but good energy about him.

Simon glanced around at the thin patronage. Everyone

else seemed too weary to harbor a negative thought.

Bobby wiped the bar with a clean rag and flipped two coasters down. "What's for breakfast?"

Chiara put her purse on the bar. "Two shots of scotch. One neat, one on the rocks."

Well, now. Simon's eyes went comically wide. No Shirley Temples for this kid, huh? He pulled a twenty out of his wallet and lay it on the bar. "Guess more of the same for me, pal."

Bobby passed Simon an appraising look before he dealt out two more coasters and a row of shot glasses, pouring straight down the line.

With a mock toast, they each knocked back the first of their shots, exhaling in appreciation of the burn.

"It's been a long time since anyone quoted Buddha to me," she said. "Makes me think there's a brain in there, after all."

"There's a brain, all right. And sometimes, it works. So." He reached for an ashtray and fished his lighter out of his pocket. "Brass tacks. Who's your master?"

"Master? I have no master." Chiara gave him an *as-if* frown. "Why? Do you have one? Who's yours?"

He shook his head and lipped his cigarette. "No, I mean, who apprenticed you? You had to learn exorcism from someone."

"Not me." She picked up the second glass and swirled it, the ice tumbling against the sides of the glass. "I was born knowing how to do that. Call it my birthright."

"Rare to meet a natural mage." He sat a little straighter in a show of respect. "Mother? Father?"

She stared down into her drink. "Both."

He let out a long, low whistle. Rarer than rare. He took several long drags on his cigarette while he thought on it. Magicians mixed like oil and water, each's own power unwilling to mingle with that of another. But to have a child together—

Big voodoo. It spoke of a will greater than power…and her power already spoke volumes.

He leaned forward to take a better look at who else was in the room. A sensation crawled up his neck as if where he should be looking was directly behind him. And he really didn't want to look, not until he had an idea what might be standing there. "You, ah, mind me asking who your folks are? Not like there's a lot of us around."

Chiara shook her head. "I don't need to tell you. Remember when I had a peek inside you? I tend to leave a trace so… I'm pretty sure you know what kind of power my father has."

He grunted and tamped out his cigarette. "Explains why I've been seeing darkness everywhere I look. No wonder I couldn't track that demon—that residue you left behind muddied everything up."

"It'll fade in a day or two." She didn't look at him. Not big on eye contact, it seemed. "But, this will help."

She rested her hand on top of his. Nothing like the first time she did it; this time, her mental touch was gentle, forgiving, a brush around the edges of his weary, sensitive mind.

He flinched, waiting for the shadowy tinge to worsen, but released a breath when things didn't go dimmer than they had been. If anything, the shade dissipated. She'd removed the remnants of the darkness she'd left behind.

"So. Your father, eh?" He slid the empty glass on its coaster back toward the inside of the bar. "I'm pretty sure I'm not going to like hearing his name."

"Which is why I'm not going to say it. Besides, I don't like to draw attention to my heritage. Let's just say he's not someone you want mad at you. He's got a hell of a temper."

Most mages did. They tended to be an emotional bunch. Simon had first-hand experience. "Fair enough," he said. "Not in the mood to fight a girl's father today, anyway."

"So." Chiara smirked. "You do possess a bit of good judgement, after all."

He shrugged. It was known to happen. "What's the story, anyway? You just bump into demons on the street and whisper them away?"

"I have—leverage. But, pretty much, yeah. I don't call myself an exorcist. That's a title people use to give validity to their flaunting of spiritual magic."

He grumbled a retort, looking away a moment. When he looked back at her, he noticed her faint smile. She was only teasing him.

"I just correct things," she said. "That's all."

"*Correct things*? I'd been tracking that demon for days when I first saw you. I didn't peg it for a mere error. He packed a lot of fire power."

"Doesn't matter their strength, their rank, their allies. They know who I have standing behind me." She sipped her drink dry before pushing the glass away, signally for another round. "Every possession is an error. Everything in the universe has its place. The dark things below, the bright things above. And the earth—that's for the spots of mortality that are still choosing their colors. It's not right for divine things to interfere. Speaking of which…"

She sighed and hooked a thumb over her shoulder. "Friend of yours?"

He twisted to look in the direction she pointed. A man leaned against the wall a few stools down from them. Mack stood motionless, inanimate, watching them with piercing, solemn eyes. "Aw, nuts. You can see him?"

"Unfortunately." She picked up her fresh drink and sipped, eyes front.

He smiled, open-mouthed in admiration. "I knew I liked you for a reason."

Mack pushed off from the wall and approached them. As he stepped into the dim light near the bar, the shadows seemed to cling to him, shadows taking the shape of long wings along his back. He laced his fingers and tented his thumbs, cupping his hands over his *dantian*, that focal point of energy that lay just below the navel—did angels even have navels?

Simon shook his head and pinched the bridge of his nose. One of those ethereal mysteries he hoped would always remain that way.

Mack spared Chiara only a quick wary glance before shaking his head. "I'm feeling a little bit like a third wheel."

Simon frowned at him. "That's usually a sign that your company isn't welcome."

"We have to talk, Simon." His voice had the quality of a bell, metallic and hollow.

"Can't it wait? I'm on a bit of a date and, angel or no angel, you're being incredibly rude to the lady here."

The angel stood taller, his shadow-wings swelling in billows as if he flexed his muscles. "I'm sure I'm not the most offensive one here."

Chiara cleared her throat. "And what would you know, bright one?"

The angel whipped a stinging look at her, his bright blue eyes flashing with challenge. "I know that someone has no shame taking payouts from the wrong side."

She faced him, undaunted. "And I know that some beings are bitter about being left out of the whole freewill scheme so take your issues and shove them where the feathers don't reach."

The angel narrowed his eyes, his mouth tilting with a cocky slant, and leaned his elbow on the bar. Dipping his face close to hers, he murmured, half seductive, half threatening. "How do you know they don't?"

She seemed to breathe deep and rear back, ready with a reply, but was interrupted when the door opened, a blade of sunlight slicing in from the street. A newcomer entered, glancing their way, lifting a chin to the bartender.

"Enough, enough." Simon hooked his arm around the angel's chest and gently pressed him back a few steps. "I really didn't figure on mediating a pissing contest so speak your piece, pal, and flutter off."

"Don't get distracted, Simon." The angel straightened his tunic. "That's all I have to say to you right now. And to you..."

Facing Chiara, he bowed. "My regards to your sire."

Chiara smirked, seeming to enjoying the farce. "And my regards to yours."

"That's the trouble with angels, isn't it?" Mack heaved a melodramatic sigh. "Always the messenger."

The newcomer walked around their side of the bar and straight into the angel, who vanished like a puff of incense.

Chiara rolled her eyes and finished her drink. "Your friend is charming."

"Not half as much as me. Just wait 'til you see me in action."

"If it's all the same, I'll pass." Chiara pulled her purse off the bar and swung her legs to the side, hopping down. "You have way too many tricks up your sleeve for my comfort."

She was leaving. His heart lobbed with sudden alarm.

No. Not yet. She couldn't leave yet. He reached out to stop her without thinking.

Her reflexes were electric. She was off the stool and an

arm's length away before he could utter his protest, her eyes flashing like lightning.

Never even saw her move.

Maybe not such a good idea to grab her. He put his hands up, hoping to placate her. "No tricks. Just—want to talk. Please."

She paused, eyeing him. "I'm not good at talking. I usually go it alone."

"And I'm sure you're more than capable. Please. Just talk. And I take back that part about a date."

Reluctantly, she sat back down. "That's a start."

"I don't meet too many people who can see him, or any angel, for that matter. Why does he know you?"

"He doesn't know me, personally. Angels can see what you are inside. He just stereotyped me, is all."

"And that whole bit about free will?" He rubbed his mouth and laughed. "Hafta admit, I rather liked seeing him choke on his feathers for once, the righteous jackass."

"Don't say that. He probably is a jackass but, then again, most angels are. It's the smugness of being securely in the Light." She toyed with the damp edge of the coaster before looking up at him. "And we need him, Simon. We need every single one of them, if we're going to keep balance. The darkness is rising, and I'm not talking a weather forecast. It's a warning."

"Now, hold on a minute—" *Darkness rising.* The words went through him like a splash of ice cold water. That phrase. It was the same that Mack used, over and over and over. Angels are defecting, the darkness is rising. Possessions are increasing, darkness is rising. Boston made the playoffs, must be the fricken darkness rising. "Why that exact phrase? Who told you?"

She pushed her drink away. "Look, it's been a long day. My correction may have looked like a bunch of simple whispering but I'm drained. Thanks for the drinks."

"I insist. Look, if I have to bind you here..." He reached into his pocket and pulled out a fistful of charms, picking through them.

She narrowed her eyes.

"If I have to *try* to bind you..." he amended, feeling a bit sheepish.

She exhaled through stiff lips as if she were trying to push away a strong impulse. "Fine. Just—put those away before someone gets hurt."

He grinned and put his gear away, hands up to show his surrender. "Better?"

"A little. But I'm going to ask the first question. What business do you have with that angel?"

Eh. Of course, she'd go right for the million-dollar question. He scratched his head and felt his way around an answer.

A child of the Light has one foot in the darkness. Mack's words echoed through his memory, a replay of a previous heraldic message. Vague enough, but he couldn't tell it to her. Not that he wouldn't, but honestly couldn't.

When he tried, a sudden alien force gripped his voice, restraining the words. The ward was a condition of the message. Kind of a divine need-to-know. And as far as Simon knew, he was the only one who needed to know.

Finally, he got something to come out of his mouth.

"It's complicated," he said.

"That much is universally understood. No? Don't want to 'talk' so much, huh?"

"It's not that. Dealing with angels can be...tricky. I don't talk to people much, either. Sometimes I forget what I can or can't say."

"A ward?" She glanced at him and nodded. "Makes sense. No worries. I know the rules. But it's not just that angel lolloping about that concerns me. It's his lolloping about a man like you."

A man like him? Comments like that were always a bit double-sided. He was more or less programed to see the dark side of things. He frowned, immediately on the defense.

But then the wall crashed in.

Literally.

His reply was lost in the barrage of glass and stone and wood that flew in all directions. He spread open his jacket, shielding Chiara and pushed her down, behind him, before scanning the scene.

The front end of a blue Ford F-150 had bellied up to the bar.

Bobby had taken the impact hard, knocked backward onto the center counter, dazed but alive. The dislodged cash register hit the floor with a clatter that was dwarfed in the shower of brick and debris pouring from the gaping hole in the wall.

A bearded man slumped out of the driver's side window, his neck bent at an ugly angle. Black smoke leaked out of his gaping mouth, his bloodied ears, and snaked its way over toward Bobby, who lay helplessly sprawled over the counter.

"No. No, no. Bobby!" Simon reached into his inside pocket, feeling for a soul-lock charm. Not there. It must have fallen out.

He boosted himself up and rolled over the bar, digging through the upset garnish tubs. Lime. Cocktail onions. Perfect for protection spells. All gone, lost in the mess of ice and glass and splintered bar.

"Simon!" Chiara was on her feet. "Get out of there before you get tagged!"

He ducked out of the way of the black vapors, stepping

a wide berth around them.

The smoke curled into Bobby's nose and mouth and the man rolled his head, rousing. His eyes blinked open. His pupils glowed a sullen red that spread and quickly engulfed the entire eye.

The voice that came out of Bobby's mouth was *not* Bobby's.

ALLIANT.

The voice was like a screech of metal under the roar of a massive waterfall. *I'VE BEEN LOOKING FOR YOU.*

Simon scrambled backward, out of reach. Bobby twitched, limbs dangling uselessly. Broken back. Not what he deserved.

Neither was a possession. Simon pushed up his sleeves and dug his thumb rings out of his front pocket. This demon was leaving. Now.

Raising his hands, he let the power of his rings connect in a flashing arc.

The demon that had taken Bobby just smiled, bloody teeth reflecting the glow of magic, a look of hungry challenge.

"No, Simon!" Chiara jumped over the bar and grabbed Simon by the sleeve, pulling him away before he could start the binding ritual. She scrambled over the debris, the smashed bar, the steaming crumpled mess of a pickup, and dragged him along behind her. "It knows you. It's tracking you."

A cold sweat broke out on his neck, his back. If it knew him—if it could track him—

Outside, a crowd was gathering, sirens grew louder, closer. He looked back at his favorite hole-in-the-wall, which was now really little more than a big hole in a wall.

The sinister black smoke crept out, mingling with the dust. Any one of those people could be the demon's next stop.

Chiara shook him. "If you want to live, Simon, you'll run."

She turned and sprinted. He didn't waste a minute in following.

Simon ran like the devil was on his heels. Maybe this time, he actually was.

They ran until they'd hit an empty alley. No innocent bystanders for a demon to possess.

She barely paused to catch her breath before tearing into him. "First angels. Now demons? What kind of friends do you keep?"

"That was no friend." Hands on his knees, he panted. He tried not to think of the sort-of could-have-almost-been friend that had lay sprawled across the counter, like a broken toy. "I don't know who that was."

"Well, that demon certainly knew you." She pushed her hair back from her face, looking very unhappy. "Come on. There's only one place it can't follow you."

Their pace brisk, they hurried several blocks south, farther away from the harbor, past Federal Hill. Once out of the tourist spotlight, the buildings became shorter and narrower. City beautification appeared to be a random thing here.

Each building had its secret. He wondered which one was keeping hers.

She rounded a corner to a one-way street and paused outside a row of triple decker homes. A weathered wooden sign over one of the front doors read ROOMS TO RENT. The sign was so old that the phone number had worn clean off. The stoop was too cracked to invite even the least discerning of vagabonds.

And God only knew why the basement window had been freshly boarded up. That alone was enough to alarm a sensible man.

Thank goodness he wasn't *that* sort. How would he ever get anything done?

"In here." She scanned the street behind them. "Hurry."

She used her shoulder to force the door, the hinges so rusted they protested and allowed only enough space for them to pass one at a time. The foyer walls were 1970s yellow ochre and peeling and hung with outdated fixtures. The single working light wavered like it would give up the ghost at any minute. Not like there was much to see, beyond the dried up leaves on the floor and old sales flyers laying shriveled and brittle in the corners.

Chiara bumped the door shut with her hind end, the wood chirping against the floor as it closed. She jerked her chin toward the staircase. "Upstairs. Third floor."

"Uh…" Simon hesitated. "Maybe you should go on up first, hon. Those stairs don't look like they'll hold both of us."

"You'd be surprised." She slung her bag over her shoulder and began to trudge up.

"Don't doubt it." He stepped onto the first and bounced a bit, testing the boards to make sure he wouldn't go crashing through. The stairs groaned but they held. His lucky day.

On the third floor, a lone door stood at the end of the hall. Definitely not the sort for a home and garden magazine cover. The bottom edge was chipped and splintered, as if something on the other side had tried to claw its way out from underneath.

Maybe it was still in there.

Chiara dug a key out of her purse and unlocked the door, her knuckles white from the exertion. The lock clacked open like a shot from a gun.

He flinched and shifted his weight to one foot to hide it.

"Well, it's not much." She pushed open the door and walked in. "But it's home."

His eyes went wide. The inside of the room was a spacious suite, floor to twenty-foot ceiling windows with heavy brocade draperies and richly furnished. Elegant tiles covered the floor beneath thick oriental rugs, orchids in antique vases.

And lamps. Looked like a lamp warehouse. Hanging lamps, Tiffanys, floor stands, table lamps, every kind imaginable. Only a few were lit, enough to illuminate the room in a homey glow. He squinted involuntarily as he imagined what it would be like if they had all been switched on. Could land a space shuttle by it, probably.

A massive black marble fireplace burned a cozy blaze. Everything, straight out of a royal estate.

Except for the couch.

It wasn't enough to say it didn't fit the rest of the décor—it positively rebelled against it. Orange upholstery that had probably seen the best Starsky and Hutch had to offer, with thin cushions that had started to develop an accidental along the edges. It probably couldn't even be called orange.

Puce. That sounded like a better fit for the mess. He wasn't even sure what puce was but he had to guess, he'd say he was looking right at it.

"You can stay the night. Time enough for the trail to go cold. I'm sure there's a room you'd find comfortable. Feel free to look around." Chiara dropped her purse onto the wretched sofa and sat down. "You are coming in, right?"

"Oh. Right." He didn't realize he was still standing in the doorway. "Is there a—"

"No barriers. No wards. Anyway. Upstairs is through there." She pointed at large arched pass-through on the far side of the room. "I've never gone through it all."

He slid his fingers into his shirt, touching the medal he wore on a chain. Pulling up layer upon layer of protection, he cracked his knuckles, rolled his shoulders, and cautiously stepped forward.

No explosion. No demon attack. No being flayed alive by booby traps.

Yet.

He side-stepped his way over to her and leaned over, peering through the doorway. A grand staircase swept up and out of sight. He'd seen some pretty intense illusions before but this was off the fricken chart.

"This glamour must be consuming a ton of power. But—" He hovered his hands near her. "Not yours. I'd feel a drain on you."

Chiara leaned back against the cushion. "That's because it's not a glamour. It's real. This place travels wherever I do. My father insists."

"Your father—"

Chiara smiled, more saccharin than sugar, and tugged off her boots. "Still don't want to talk about him."

"But this would take infinite strength to sustain."

"You really don't grasp the concept of infinity, do you?"

He chuckled. "What's not to grasp? Big. Really damn big."

"Okay, give me one good example of something infinite."

"Easy." He clamped a cigarette between his lips and lit a

tinder stick from the fireplace. "The universe."

"Seriously?"

"Yeah, seriously."

"The universe is anything but infinite. Matter can neither be created nor destroyed, remember? Even humans know that."

"But it's expanding."

"Expansion doesn't make it infinite. There is still a limit. The front of the storm, the leading edge. That limit keeps it from being infinite."

He sat on a satin lowboy near the mantelpiece and flicked his ashes into the fireplace. "So, Dr. Hawking, what is infinite, then?"

Chiara shrugged. "Humans."

Simon chuffed out a lungful of smoke and barked a laugh. "Humans, my dear, are the very definition of the word limit. The antithesis of infinite."

"That's where you're wrong. The human mind is infinite. There is no limit to a man's dreams, or hopes, or despairs. The imagination, the fear, the desperate wishes could overfill a bottomless well and drown the lot of us. That's why this war will be so bad. It will be fought on the battlegrounds of man's infinity. That's why I need to make these corrections. The darkness has an unfair advantage. Hell isn't much one for rules and their players keep going off sides."

"So, you kick them back into line with your corrections."

"So do you. You just don't realize the scope of the game you're playing."

"That damned angel, though." He thumbed the filter, staring at the ember. "He does."

"Yeah. You can bet he does. And—I know it's not worth much, but...I'm sorry."

"For what?"

"For what you're carrying around inside." Before he could reply, she pointed toward the staircase once more. "Go find a soft bed and get some sleep, Simon."

For the first time in years, morning didn't arrive like a right hook to the jaw. Maybe because for the first time in years, he'd slept in an actual bed.

He lay a while without stirring, watching the sunlight slowly shift itself across the bedspread. A pillow. How could a sock full of fluff make such a difference in a man's outlook on the new day?

The half-bath off the bedroom didn't boast more than a mirror and a scented square of soap, but even that left him feeling like a slice of spring. By the time he made his way downstairs, he felt ready to take on the world. Perhaps a bit of the otherworld, as well.

Chiara lay curled on the sofa, that ugly rickety old thing, staring at the fire. She sat up when she saw him.

"And I thought I was an early riser." He trotted down the last few steps and bee-lined over to the fireplace. He'd left his smokes on the mantelpiece overnight. That was as quit as he ever wanted to get. "I've been nosing around. Hope you don't mind. I like to look in the corners, if you know what I mean. Especially in rooms that shouldn't exist. Did you know there's a swimming pool?"

"A pool, yes. But it's not the swimming kind."

"Where you down here all night?"

Chiara nodded.

"I saw at least a dozen bedroom suites up there, at least. Don't you sleep?"

"Sometimes. But only if I have to."

Simon lit his cigarette and waved a hand at the ratty couch. "Why not something a little more aesthetic? Or at least less fire sale?"

"This is mine." She ran her hands over the fraying cushion. "It's ugly, I know. But it's mine. It's actually what was in my room the first time everything got…upgraded. I like something organic. Does that word make sense? Just something I know is real. This couch, this exact location where it sits, it's actually physical. Real. I don't stray beyond these dimensions very often."

He thought about the fact that he'd just slept upstairs in a room that shouldn't exist. If she didn't go up there… "But you can, right?"

"I can go lots of places. I simply choose not to."

"So the pool upstairs doesn't see much action?"

She rubbed her hands and looked away. "Not if I can help it."

"So would you mind if I…?" He pointed over his shoulder. "I didn't exactly pack my trunks."

"I think you'd be happier if you stick to the, ummm… " She looked upwards, thinking. "…hot tub, instead."

"There's a hot tub?"

"Maybe. Go look for one. You'll like the bubbles."

He winked at her and rubbed his palms together. "Bubbly is my middle name."

By noontime, his belly had got the best of him. Towel-dried, his hair was a lump of damp waves that made him look twelve years old. Not the imposing look for a master of Arcanum.

The one thing he hadn't found while snooping through her place was a kitchen. The least he could do, he figured, was offer to buy her lunch. His favorite place was a diner by the river. Definitely a "locals only" kind of spot.

"First," he said. "I need to make a quick stop."

Adjacent to the diner was a parking lot, its pavement

cracked, crumbled, and reduced to dirt in many places. Bushes had grown through the chain link fence bordering the back edge. Looked like a place you'd only park on a dare.

On the far end, a faded blue late model Chevy Astro was backed into a parking space. The front tire was booted, the dingy windshield littered with tickets.

Chiara wrinkled her nose and bounced a few suspicious glances off it.

"Aw, hell," he said. "The cloaking spell wore off again."

Going around to the back, he ran his finger over the lock, muttering. He pulled open the door to reveal a make-shift living space: the last row of seats had been pulled out to store open duffle bags stuffed with rumpled clothing, a scattering of camp cooking implements. Several steamer trunks took up most of the space.

He watched her survey the interior, make the connection. Well, if she had any doubts, she could always take a look in the windows. Pretty sure she'd see the blanket rolled up on the back seat.

Not that he slept here much. Not that he slept anywhere much. Magic was better than caffeine for all that.

"I just need to pick up a few supplies." He pulled one of the duffle bags closer and rummaged through it. "And freshen up, if you don't mind. I hadn't packed an overnight bag and your, ah, apartment wasn't equipped for male company."

He turned to a small mirror hanging on rear door. Chiara poked around at the nearest box, lifting the lid. He eyed her a moment, but didn't stop her. If she wanted to look at his magician's workshop, so be it. What would she care about books and vials and herbs? Natural mages had no need for such tawdry tricks.

Chiara clinked through the bottles, lifting one up and peering into its questionable contents. "You're a travelling show, like the vaudeville folk I remember growing up."

"I'll have you know it's all quite authentic, thank you." He grabbed a cordless razor and began to shave. "One hundred percent snake oil free."

"Mmm." She closed the lid and pushed the box back enough so she could sit in the bay. "So this is where you live."

"I don't live anywhere." Dropping his razor into the bag, he located a hair brush and a stick of deodorant. "My home is the open road. Sometimes, quite literally."

She turned her back, giving him a little privacy.

He eyed her. Manners, after all. Don't often see that in an exorcist. They tended to be a bossy lot, especially the well-funded, natural kind.

She swung her feet. "Home is where you hang your hat."

"Don't like hats." He reached behind her and flipped open a small metal box. Another thing he didn't care if she saw. Just his piggy bank. Rolls, wads, rubber-banded stacks. He shuffled through the loose bills and took a few, flipping the box shut again. "But I do like all-day breakfast. Come on."

She hopped down so he could shut the doors. "Aren't you going to lock it?"

"I'll do one better." Raising his hands, he chanted a few lines. It was a dead language, but it still held power. He pulled a thin stick from his pocket.

"What's that?"

"Chicory. Grows like weeds around here." He pointed behind him, where the blue flowers straggled along the fence line of the parking lot. He'd harvested enough to last a long time. One of the reasons why he parked the van here. "In addition to being a very manly type of flower, it's a magical aid."

Flicking his lighter, he set the tip aflame. The stick sizzled and incinerated into a puff of smoke.

Chiara watched him, wearing an amused expression. She pointed to the boot. "What are you going to do about that?"

"What I always do. Fast talk my way out of it." He jerked his head toward the diner. "Come on."

Perhaps three feet from the van, they passed through a shimmery border. Chills raced down between his shoulders as he crossed through the ward. Something he never got used to—a prickly kind of shiver that both thrilled and terrified him. Just a little. Not that he'd ever admit it to anyone.

He shook it off. Once on the other side, the van vanished from their sight.

"See? Invisibility from a weed. Will magical wonders never cease?" He smoothed his hair once more. "We've fed the meter, love. Time to feed us."

Chiara wasn't hungry.

She never really was. One of the perks of being part divinity.

Or maybe not. Simon was working his way through a pot of coffee and his second plate of waffles, seeming to enjoy every crowded mouthful, yet devouring the food like it was his last meal. Such urgency, such hurry, such relish.

All she did was push pieces of cantaloupe around a plate with her fork. Maybe not a perk at all. She scowled. Better not to think that way.

She glanced around the diner. Simon had said it was a favorite spot of his. Suited him—casual, loud, a little rumpled around the edges. Very human. Very temporary, and not seeming to mind in the least.

It was strange, sitting in a place like this, as if she were just an ordinary person having an everyday meal. Strange but...nice.

And "nice" was a welcomed change.

"How you doing with coffee, Murph?" The waitress stopped at their table and lifted the pot. "I'll bring you a fresh one. You okay with your juice, hon?"

Chiara just nodded. The glass was almost full.

"Okay, you need anything, just holler." The waitress winked at Simon before walking away.

"Strange to hear them call you Murphy." Chiara took a shy glance at his face and tilted her head. "You don't look like a Murphy."

"How many Murphys you know?"

"In Baltimore or in general?" She blinked innocently at him. "I did spend some time in County Wexford before the Great Migration. Murphys all over the place."

He shook his head. "Great Migration. I have a feeling you're trying to date yourself. Quit it. I'm trying to act like hot young chicks hang out with me all the time. Don't wreck the illusion."

She chuckled and took a tentative bite of cantaloupe. Such a bright, summery taste. And mortals ate like this every day. How did they possibly stand the pleasure?

The television blared behind her on the counter. Local news. She tilted her head, trying to capture another part of this moment, this everyday world.

"Local authorities have been asking residents to notify police if they have seen this man."

Simon had looked up, his eyes turning to stone. She craned her head to look at what caught his attention.

The TV flashed a picture of a shaggy-looking young man, bleached-blond hair with dark roots, scruffy jaw. Chin tipped a little too high to be humble. A name and number in choppy block letters most likely cropped out from beneath his face.

A mugshot. Of him.

He swore under his breath.

"Simon Alliant, formerly of Boston, has been thought to be living in the Eastern US and has been spotted near Baltimore. He is wanted for questioning. Please call—"

The station turned to white snow static.

She whipped her head back in time to see him lower his hand before sullenly stabbing at his breakfast. He solved everything with his magic, didn't he?

The waitress heard the noise and picked up the remote, switching the channels, before retreating to her newspaper at the end of the counter.

Chiara waited until the girl was out of earshot. "That was you."

He didn't look up. "In all my mid-nineties flannel-shirted glory."

"What do the police want?"

"What they always want, I suppose." He topped off his coffee. "Peace, order, a chance to put on the riot gear."

"What do they want with you?"

Simon met her eyes, rubbing his mouth, looking as if he were trying to decide what to say. He could be chatty when he wanted to be, but she had already formed several impressions of him. One of those impressions was mule-headed stubbornness.

"I owe you a truth," he said at long last. "Because you showed me a kindness last night by taking me in. I don't share my truths easily so I—" He choked to a stop and took a hasty gulp of coffee.

She waited, not rushing him. Gone was the cocky swagger. He was so close to talking. She didn't want to spook him.

"I've recently become an orphan. My mom. Ah. She's dead."

It didn't carry a particularly mournful tone. "Did you kill her?"

"What? Christ, you're a dark one." He pushed back against the booth. It creaked under the sudden shift of weight. "No, I didn't kill my mother."

She reached for his hand, her heart heavy with compassion. "Simon, I'm sorry. I had to ask. Why do the police want to question you? Are you in trouble?"

"When am I not in trouble?"

"That was a mug shot."

He slipped his hand out of her grasp. "It was."

"But you were seriously young in that picture."

"Strangely, I'm not flattered."

"Listen. I don't judge. That's not my division, okay? And I already know you've had dark times in your past. What is coming back to haunt you now?"

"Nothing's coming back. It's always been here."

"I'm very sorry you lost your mother. It's not easy, losing a parent. Were you with her?"

"No, no, she...she was back home. Up north. She'd been in a personal care home. No matter, she wouldn't have known me, anyway. She'd parted ways with reality a long time ago."

"That must have been hard, getting a call like that when you're so far away."

"I didn't get a call. Nobody left to call me." He sloshed fresh coffee into his half-full cup. "Nobody knows where I am. I left home and went to college, then dropped out first semester, then fell right off the edge of the planet. Couldn't stand knowing what I'd done to her."

She leaned forward, trying to press the truth out of him. "What did you do?"

"I'm the one who drove her insane. Like everything else, it's my fault. Anyway. The cops prolly just want me to pop in to sign some papers, take care of the house, that sort of thing. Legalities."

"Then why show a mug shot photo?"

"It's the only photo that still exists of me. And those things never go out of style."

Simon stood and dug the wad of bills out of his front pocket, peeling out singles and dropping them on the table. He picked up the check and turned to look for the waitress. She wasn't the one to catch his eye.

Mack stood at the far wall, next to the restrooms. Giving Simon a deliberate look and a slight nod, he disappeared into the men's room. If anyone else had done that, it would have been creepy.

He thought about it a moment. Nah. Angel or no, it was still creepy.

"Why don't you take this?" Simon handed Chiara the bill and the money. "Go settle our tab. I need to heed a call of nature."

"Fine. I'll wait outside for you."

He headed into the lavatory. Leaning, he scanned under the stalls. It was empty except for the angel, standing in front of one of the urinals.

Simon stepped up beside him and unzipped. "I'm dying to look over, you know."

"That would be rude."

"I didn't think angels had those sort of workings."

Mack sighed and raised his chin, closing his eyes. "Part of our ethereal mystery."

"Make it quick. I don't want to stand here all day holding my—"

Mack turned and looked at him. "A Ladder approaches. Two days from now. I anticipate something...substantial."

"That's all? You didn't have to drag me into the men's room to tell me that. There's something else."

"Just walk away from her," Mack said. "She's a straight line to trouble. Go right out the back door and make some distance."

"I don't think I like you telling me what to do."

"I don't tell you what to do very often."

Simon stowed his gear and zipped, bouncing on one leg to settle himself. "You don't tell me even when I ask you to."

"I'm telling you now. Walk away from her."

"I don't walk away from allies. We're on the same side of this fricken war of yours."

"Don't fool yourself into believing that." Mack leveled a stern gaze at him. "She's not one of us. She's definitely not one of you. She is on her own side."

"Doesn't really come across as the selfish sort."

"She's not. She's just not fighting the same war."

"Light versus dark?" Simon crossed his arms. "Everything she's said to me sounds fresh out of your playbook."

"You just don't get it, do you?"

"Look. All I know is it's fricken hard, being on the front lines. Fighting demons. Abusers of magic and forces blacker than pitch. Shamans and necromancers and soul hunters. Everything from the mortal plane down." Simon pointed at the door, out toward the girl-exorcist-whatever who had saved his butt just the day before. Mack hadn't pulled him out of the way of that demon. Chiara had. "For once, it's nice bumping in to a person who isn't trying to bring about the ruin of souls. And, by the way—she's told me more about the darkness rising in one night that you have in three years."

"I didn't realize you were so blind." Suddenly, Mack smiled. It was eerie because Simon knew he didn't have a sense of humor. "You haven't figured out what she is yet."

"You mean who."

"No. I don't."

The door swung open and a burly man hustled in, heading for the lone stall, one hand working his belt, and slamming the door shut behind him. Time to evacuate. The shit was about to hit.

Mack was already gone.

Diesel fumes, hydraulic whines, and annoying loud cell phone conversations. Three cheers for the public transportation system. The bus lifted from the curb and lurched forward in a stomach-shuddering surge.

Simon blew out hard and sat back, swallowing. Nausea. He'd almost forgotten the nausea. Hip, hip, hooray for buses.

Chiara eyed him suspiciously a moment, her gaze lingering even when he tried to wave it off. "I've never had anyone tag along before."

Her voice held a tone of distinct amusement. Simon leaned over to where she sat in the row in front of him. Despite the motion sickness, he preferred the back seat of the bus. No one to sneak up behind him.

Plus, he got extra leg room when sitting in the middle seat. A good stretch was just what he wanted. That, and privacy if he needed to hurl. "Not one to pass up a field trip. I just want to observe, is all. Watch what you do. How you do it."

She shifted sideways to face him, avoiding his sprawled out legs. "I thought you knew it all already."

"You just think I know it all."

She shook her head, laughing. "More like I think you think you know it all."

"Same difference. But, naw. No such thing as a master in this line of work. Never stop learning, never stop discovering. Every corner you turn offers something you never saw before, a way to reach a bit further."

"What's the endgame?"

He sat back. "I really hope there isn't one."

"Why?"

"Because, whatever it is, it can't be good."

He stretched his arms out along the back of the seats. Perfect time to change the topic. Musing about his mortality and eventual horrid demise was a mood killer. "Good choice for a demon hunting trip," he said. "Nothing like public transportation to bring out the worst in someone."

She leaned over the seat and poked him, playfully, before turning back to survey the passenger. Her head tilted, a bird on alert. Slowly she raised her hand and pointed to a young man sitting halfway up the bus on a side seat.

Simon sat forward, elbows on his knees, and looked up at her face before following the line of her finger.

"Him." Eyes trained on the boy, she nodded. "Do you see them?"

"See what?"

"The shadows inside him."

Simon slipped the scrying lens out of his pocket and peered through it. The guy didn't look any different than anyone else. He shook his head. "He's normal."

"He's an open door, an unholy invitation," she said. "Demons use people like him. They're easy to breech. All people have to do is embrace the light, make good choices, and they'd squash the shadows. There'd be no chink in their armor."

He palmed the lens and sat back, with a quick jerk of his head, disagreeing. "I've seen enough child possessions to disagree."

"Would you?" She turned back to him and peered into his eyes. "You think that children are incapable of harboring shadows?"

"They are the innocents."

Chiara snorted. "Hardly. Okay, some are. But they are human and, as children, they lack the moral training, the life experience to know the difference between right and wrong. They're basically psychopaths."

He barked out a laugh that squeezed his belly more than what was comfortable. "Oh, I bet you're a real trip at kids' parties."

"I wouldn't know. Never been to one."

"How dreary a childhood you must have had."

"You assume I had one." She shifted in her seat, reaching across the aisle to grasp the back of the seat across from her, as if bracing him for a sudden stop. "Look. He's changing. Get ready."

He raised the scrying lens again. Nothing. What did she see? "What's going on?"

A subtle change swept over the boy, like a wave of chills travelling down his body. It left a sullen red glow in its wake.

"Aw, fricken a." Simon lowered the glass. The kid was going to manifest, right now, on a bus full of people.

"I told you he's an open door, didn't I?" Chiara glanced back at him. "Well, something on the other side just got really curious."

Simon instinctively reached into his shirt, feeling for his amulet, and drew a breath. It was going to take a big spell to keep the others on the bus from seeing a demon manifest. And everyone knew, what you can't see can't hurt you.

Most of the time. He couldn't stop that last sarcastic thought.

He murmured the first words of a Macedonian protection spell.

"Shh." Chiara stayed his hand and put a hand over his mouth. "I'll do this. It's best it doesn't notice you."

Simon pulled her hand off. "So what if it does?"

The look she gave him would have stopped a waterfall in its tracks. "Angels aren't the only messengers."

She pulled the stop cord and stood, smoothing her skirt over her hips, and sauntered up the aisle, smiling flirtatiously. There wasn't a single soul that didn't look up and stare. Dragging her fingers against his shoulder, she swiveled her head and crooked her finger at the guy before moving to the front exit, a world of wiggle in her walk.

The kid sprang from the seat followed her up the aisle

like a dog as the bus slowed to a jerky stop at the corner.

"Aw, hell." Simon slipped out the rear door and scanned the sidewalk, not wanting to lose visual contact.

Not to worry. She was easy to spot. They'd already started up the street. She bounced along beside the host, giving him full view of her feminine assets, and tugged him toward a side street. It would take an iron will to ignore her. He'd vouch personally for that.

A twenty-year-old guy with a head full of hormones had little room to spare for an iron will. Fed by the host's lust, the demon continued to manifest. A slightly acrid odor tinged the heavy city smells of exhaust and subway. Chiara drew him away from the bulk of people, flirting and smiling, twirling her hair, licking her lips, and lured him around the corner.

Simon blew out a tight breath. Hell, he would have followed her, even if he hadn't been hunting with her. He kept a cool distance and did his best to watch only the kid.

Jesus, that was really hard to do.

He stayed at the corner, lens up to his eye, monitoring the manifestation while trying to remain unnoticed. That was hard, too. UNNOTICEABLE just wasn't his thing.

Halfway down the deserted service street, Chiara swung the boy's hand and leaned in close to him, whispering to him, a smile on her lips like she was talking dirty to him.

But it wasn't the start of a steamy hook-up. It was the beginning of a battle.

The demon-struck kid struggled, straining to get away from her. She never broke a sweat. Her actions were smooth and calm, as if there were no conflict at all. She gripped the host's wrists, eyes locked with his, commanding his attention.

The wind shifted toward Simon and he inhaled, sniffing the air. An ionic bite stung his nose, making him rub it.

The air felt heavy with the oppression of charged power.

This demon was fighting back. And that couldn't be good.

Her voice became a little louder, more insistent. He could finally hear what she always seemed to be whispering.

"You know your place. Your place is below. Go back to your place below." Chiara repeated the phrase, chanting in smooth firm tones.

Simon ruffled his hair and shifted his weight, from one foot to the other and back, uncomfortable with the whole thing. The power discharge, the unwillingness of the demon to give it up. His chest felt like he'd been straitjacketed, tight and anxiety-ridden. COME ON, COME ON, COME ON—

He flexed his fingers, itching for something to hold. His "worry stick", for example. A nice, powerful, magic-packed wand, one that had a kick like a double-barrel shotgun.

No, no. He stuffed his hands in his pockets to still them. No good. His Peruvian binding rings were in there and it would be so easy to slip them on...

No. He crossed his arms, pinning his hands under his armpits. She said not to use a charm. He had to trust her. But dammit, this was taking too long—

The demon issued a low growl that rolled out like summer thunder. It wasn't going to give up. Its agitation was nearly palpable. The ground under its feet began to crack and split, the air shimmering as it gave off heat. The demon snarled and snapped its teeth at her, the host's lips distorted and pulled back inhumanly thin.

She didn't even seem to notice how critical things just got. Or didn't care—

Simon paced like a caged wolf, watching them,

scanning the busy street behind him. If this demon let loose, no telling how many people would get hurt.

Suddenly, the kid broke the hold she had on his wrists. With a strike almost too fast to follow, it grabbed Chiara by the throat and lifted her. The tips of her toes scraped the pavement.

That was it. Line was crossed. He couldn't wait a second longer. Sliding his fingers into his shirt, he reached for his amulet. The Macedonian protection charm would still work from a distance.

The moment his fingers made contact, the amulet sparked. He snapped his fingers away, blowing on them to cool the sting. Too much demonic energy in the air.

The demon whipped its head around, spotting Simon. It raised its free hand and pointed at him. Its mouth opened and a roar of voices screamed out. IS THAT WHY YOU BRING HIM?

WAIT. Simon had heard that voice before. The demon who'd taken Bobby. The one who had said his name.

Chiara seemed too busy trying to pry its fingers from around her throat to answer. She rolled her eyes toward Simon, her look heavy with reprimand.

The demon lowered its chin like a bull on the charge and curled its empty hand into fist. It drew Simon closer, pulling him with the sheer force of his power.

Simon scrabbled, dug in his heels, almost plowing up the ground, unable to fight.

With the demon's attention diverted, Chiara finally broke its grip. Rubbing her throat, she backed out of reach, a wary eye on Simon. "You have a choice. Balazog never told you, did he?"

Horror slammed into Simon like a train. He sputtered and wind-milled his arms, a new desperation in his attempt to escape the demon's grasp. All the heat drained from him, a cold buzz washing down his limbs. "Bala— Chiara, get out of here. He's—"

"He's going to make a smart choice. Aren't you?" Chiara stepped between the demon and the man. "Because you have quite a selection of choices to choose from."

She started to tick off her fingers.

"You can leave the way you came and close the door behind you." She wiggled her thumb. "Relatively painless choice."

She raised her index finger next. "I can force you out—and you know I can. Might hurt, much to my own regret, since you've never personally done me any wrong."

She twisted her wrist, displaying three fingers, and regarded the demon with a thin-lipped glare. "Or, I can have this man here shove you out with his chanting and smoke and—" She sniffed the air and shrugged. "Mandrake root, it would seem. Doesn't look like much, I know, but he's got power. And that makes the third option a relatively painful choice."

Laughing, the demon dropped its grip on Simon and swiveled its head toward her, like a cobra in sway.

YOU THINK THIS ONE HAS ANY POWER? CHARLETAIN. SCHOOL BOY. WEAK.

Chiara circled the host, ignoring him. "Or...I suppose we can call my father, and he'll show you the error of your ways. And that will be the most excruciating choice of all. I guarantee it."

The demon-infested man huffed out a big breath, smoke curling out of his nose. ALL THIS TALK OF CHOICE. WE HAVE NO CHOICE. WE HAVE NO WILL OF OUR OWN.

"Speak for yourself," she said.

YOU ARE A DISAPPOINTMENT TO HIM.

"Don't presume to know him...or me. And insulting me

really isn't the way to go." She raised her hands. No longer ticking choices off her fingers, she splayed both hands, which took on an eerie glow, as if flames rolled beneath the surface of her skin. "And I may have understated myself. The 'me option' is really going to hurt."

The demon stepped backwards. CHIARO—

"Shhhh," she hissed. "No more talking."

She lunged, grabbing the host by the shoulder and driving him back against the wall. She slapped her other hand onto his forehead. The sounds of searing flesh, a wet sizzle like a steak on a hot grill, made Simon's stomach quiver.

The demon screamed and fought, shaking, thrashing, convulsing. But it was no match for the lady, whose eyes blazed as fiercely as had the palms of her hands. The demon struggled but failed to shake loose from her grip.

Chiara grimaced and pushed the host to its knees.

The host threw back his head and wailed, a moan of a multitude of voices. A swirl of black fog slithered out of his open mouth, bellowing out into a swirling column of sullen heat and pitch-black smoke. It condensed into a dark, rumbling mass that tumbled into and upon itself until it disappeared with a thunderclap and a retina-searing flash.

The host collapsed. Clean. Exorcised.

Surprisingly, still alive.

Chiara picked up his baseball hat and tossed it down at him.

The kid pushed up on his hands, looking around, confused. "What happened?"

She squatted beside him, tin in hand. Without answering, she smeared the jelly on his head, then into his eyes, mouth, ears, everywhere.

He sputtered and pushed her hands away. "What the

hell are you doing, lady?"

Standing, she glared down at him. "You were possessed, you fool, and it was your own damned fault. I suggest you find a church, confess your sins, and find the good in your heart before Hell takes you for good. And I promise, they'll do more than burn your face."

The jelly sizzled and smoked, smelling like burned hair and incense. He groaned and gingerly reached up to his face.

"Remember that pain," she said. "It's just a taste of what an eternity of Hell will feel like if you don't find the light." She coldly turned away and left the boy on the ground, and left Simon staring holes in her back as she walked away.

Stubborn fool.

Chiara busied herself with a handkerchief, wiping the last of the chrism from her fingers. If she wasn't careful, she'd accidentally rub her eyes or something and then it would really burn.

She scowled, thinking about that young man. It would only be a matter of time before he opened himself up to darkness again. All the chrism in the world wouldn't be enough to burn the stupidity out of him.

And for all the demons to break through—

Chiara couldn't make herself look at Simon. She knew that he knew. This one little possession just pushed the two of them through a doorway she knew she'd never find her way back through. She didn't want that with him.

She didn't want that for him.

It wouldn't do any good to walk away, not now. But there was nothing wrong with trying.

Simon followed silently behind her. She could sense his turmoil, sullen and brooding, a storm beneath the surface.

At least he waited until they were safely out of sight of the passersby before he closed the distance between them and spun her around to face him.

She didn't expect to see all that suspicion, heavy and accusing, glaring back at her from behind his pointed finger.

"You banished that demon with hellfire."

Chiara looked away and shrugged away from him. What could she say, besides yes, I did.

"And not just any old demon, now, was it? That was a minion of Bal—" He broke off, unable to say it. "He serves a general. Of Hell. And you used hellfire on him. Of all the—"

He was sputtering mad. "You don't just get to throw that stuff around. I think there's a story you mean to tell me."

"Is that what you want?" She spread her hands, suspecting nothing she could say would make him feel any better. "A story? I've got a universe full of them."

"You're sassy, sweetheart, but it's not enough to get you out of this. What are you? Demon?"

Her lips curled in disdain. "As if. If I were demon, don't you think your angel buddy would have drawn on me?"

"Backstory, then. " Simon regarded her shrewdly and slowly nodded his head. "And I will have it. I just don't know what I want you to tell me first. Do I ask about how you came to wield hellfire? Or do I go right to the heart of what's bugging me and ask why do you know that demon?"

She rubbed her brows. Why did this man have to be so damnably curious? It had been ages since she even tried to connect with another human being. He was special. He was...open-minded. But no one could be that accepting. Not considering the truths she held.

Not even the man who stared at her now, the man with pockets full of charms and secrets and an unforgiveable past. She saw the resolve in his eyes, the demand for answers.

"Okay, you want to know?" She swallowed hard. "First, swear your silence."

Simon rolled his eyes. "Fine, fine. I solemnly swear—"

Flippant man. Have mortal men truly lost respect for an oath? He needed to be encouraged to take this seriously.

She lowered her barriers, the ones that hid her divinity from humans, and allowed her power to physically manifest. Her eyesight dimmed as the power surged, causing her eyes to glow.

"Not words, Simon." She bared her teeth, her voice rumbling into a growl. The power was a thing of its own, a force that disdained mortal control. "Swear. With your soul."

His eyes grew wide and he backed up a step. Was he afraid? Would he run? Her resolution stumbled. Why did it bother her that he might? Her barriers sulked back up, as if she were ashamed for him to see her, as if she stood bare before his scrutiny.

He didn't run. He just stared at her, hard, and set his jaw.

For a moment she thought he'd reach for one of his innumerable charms, the pocketful of magic he carried around like so much change.

But he surprised her.

He merely nodded. "I give you my solemn word."

She felt the words when he spoke them. He hadn't even reached for an amulet. His oath had bourn a solid conviction and a silent trace of magic enforcing it.

Hmm. Just shy of a blood oath. She released a breath she hadn't realized she'd been holding. Suddenly, he had new value, most deserving of a reassessment.

"I have a lofty heritage," she said.

"I'm listening."

"I'm...Enochian."

That made his eyebrows shoot up. He rocked back on his heels and shoved his hand deep into his trouser pockets. "Well. You now have my full and riveted attention. The Enochians were the offspring of angels and humans. But they don't wield hellfire."

"True. But only my mother was Enochian. My father..."

"Ah." Long silence. "The darkness you left behind when you riffled through my brain."

Yes. The darkness she left behind. As much as she tried to distance herself from it, that particular aspect of herself wasn't something she could simply turn off.

"I assumed he was a dark mage, which would give you that oily stain." He chewed the side of his thumb.

Oily stain. It made her feel...soiled. Wounded, she lowered her eyes. "If that's what you want to call it."

"But he isn't a mage, is he? That darkness comes from demonic influence. No wonder you said I know him. I'm a demonologist." He spit to the side. "Of course I would. So. A half-demon who exorcises demons. That's a new one."

"Don't trivialize it." She couldn't keep the edge out of her voice.

"There's no possible way to trivialize any of this. Are you out of your mind? You have a direct connection to hell. You can't go making enemies like this, especially not that one."

"I'm not afraid of him."

"You should be. No wonder Mack was ruffled when he saw you. You shouldn't even exist. Angel blood, and demon—it's not a matter of disagreeing on holiday plans. It's bad chemistry. Plain and simple."

"I have a purpose, Simon. I know what I have to do.

I've never shied away from it. I know you find me...an abomination—"

"Now, wait." His whole demeanor changed. "I never said that."

"You don't have to. I see it in your eyes. There is so much in your eyes, Simon. Such despair, such guilt. Such condemnation for what you see as a failure in another person."

He looked away, a shadow casting down over his expression. Hurt and trying to hide it.

But not for long. He rolled his shoulders and slowly looked back at her.

"I just watched you exorcize an officer of Balazog Corinthian," he said." A demon of no small influence. And you did it without even breaking a sweat. If we're gonna work together, I think I deserve to know who I'm working with. You really need to tell me who your father is."

Not a chance, on this plane or any other. "My father is a collector. A connoisseur of the strange and wonderful and impossible and damned. And one of the things he collects is offspring. He's not really a family man. Bad relationship with his own father, I guess. Left him with screwed up family values. He chose my mother because of her exquisite genetics. They probably should have tried to get to know each other a little first before jumping into the whole parenthood thing."

"You're a divinity. I gotta be honest. I'm having a hard time wrapping my brain around it, and my brain is stretchier than most. Half demon, half Enochian—"

"I am mortal." Her voice went nearly hoarse with conviction. At least in part. These days, more theory than anything else. "There is a piece of me that is mortal, a piece that is all my own. And that is why I fight to keep humanity free of divine influence. I fight because I know how precious mortality is. All these corrections—it kicks the power back to where it belongs but it's just not enough. I cannot make them unsee what they saw. I cannot make them forget what it feels like to be a divinity."

He nodded and dropped his head. "I can."

She turned. "What?"

With a sigh, he met her gaze. "I said, I can. I can make them forget. And I do. When I complete an exorcism, I cast a little follow-up disremember spell. It's easy, actually."

He shrugged. "A rapid hypnotic induction, a few words of a spell I learned in Guatemala and a pinch of mandrake root under their tongue. I mean, I've just ripped a demon out of their body, out of their psyche. They are usually quite open to suggestion after an experience like that."

"And..." She pulled at her lower lip, thinking. She never thought it possible. Memories were part of a mortal; embedded with scents and sounds and emotions. So many parts of the human brain were wired for memory storage, making it difficult to isolate any one spot. From a scientific view, erasing a memory was complicated. From an emotional standpoint, it was probably impossible. Even the things a person thought they forgot could resurface with the right trigger, conscious or unconscious. "You do that to every one you exorcise?"

He scratched his hair, ruffling it. "More or less. Some guys, they might be useful. I let them keep the experience if I think they're worth it."

"Worth what?"

"Joining the fray. I'm not the only mortal out there fighting. I don't know too much about the big wigs, now. They have their own organization and rules and credit union memberships. I'm a bottom feeder, a freelancer. I just kick a new recruit their way every now and then."

She mused, staring at the fire until it was a blur, lost deep in her own thoughts. "So that's where the money comes from. You get a... referral fee."

Simon suddenly smiled, cheeky and wide.

"Clever girl, you are. You didn't think I made a dishonest living, did you?" He shook his head. "Show a girl your mug shot and she never forgets it."

The sky was mottled with thick clumps of cloud swatches of deep blue peeping out in spots. Simon shifted the van into park on the side of a long stretch of highway, scanning the tree line. This felt like the right spot. Mack's angelic GPS was usually right on.

Chiara squinted in the same direction. "What are you doing?"

"Watching. Mack said he'd be here." He pushed up his sleeve to check his watch. Okay, more than watch. Also had compass orientation: the usual N-S-E-W, latitude, longitude, planetary positions. YOU KNOW, he'd say. THE BASICS. At any rate, he was in the right place at the right time.

A shaft of sunlight suddenly pierced the cloud cover, sending down a broad, shining stream.

"Ah, knew it was coming." He grinned. "You can smell it."

She sniffed experimentally. "I don't smell anything out of the ordinary."

"Of course, you can't. You're a divinity. It would be like trying to smell your own breath. Now, come on."

He hopped out of the van, lighting a stick of chicory and tossing the smoking twig over his shoulder. Without even a glance behind him, he jogged across the grass toward the trees, heading toward the spot where the shifting beams of sunlight pulsed and shone down like a shimmering curtain.

"Where are you going?" She called after him, carefully stepping through the grass behind him.

"You wanted to see what Mack's all about," he said. "This is the perfect explanation."

He led her through the thin scrub of birch and laurel bushes, using the bright sky as a compass.

"I don't understand." Chiara stooped to avoid the thin branches that picked at her, snagging her hair like nasty little fingers. "We're following the sunshine?"

"Not just any old sunshine," Simon called over his shoulder at her. "That's a Jacob's Ladder. Quaint Bible story, you'll remember; Jacob fell asleep on a stone and dreamed of a great golden ladder, upon which angels ascended and descended. He called it a Gateway to Heaven. Later on, the Christ recognized the brilliance of the imagery and referred to himself as the Divine Ladder."

They emerged from the woods at a patch of meadow, open field. Less than a hundred yard away, the sunbeams fell upon the grass in a sunny puddle. Quite like finding the end of the rainbow, gold and all. He glanced over at her, interested in seeing her reaction.

Chiara's mouth made a tiny O of wonder.

Grinning, he dug a cigarette out of the pack and crumpled the wrapper. "Thing is, it wasn't a dream, and it wasn't a ladder. Jacob was the son of Isaac, son of Abraham. Living descendant of the man who made a covenant with God. As such, he was aware of the existence of a real, living god and that knowledge causes the ability to see divinities. Angels. What he saw was a shaft of light, just like that one, and the angels that traverse it."

"Mother talked about angels, the stories her ancestors told. The Ladder is the only connection between Heaven and Earth, just as a hell gate is the only connection between Hell and Earth."

"Hell gates have never been proven to exist." He raised a lecturing finger toward her. "I have it on good authority."

"You need proof to believe in something?"

"Actually, I do." Simon nodded. "We'll agree to disagree on the gate thing but you're right about the Ladder. It's how earth-bound angels communicate with the boys upstairs."

"So Mack can get up to Heaven on that shaft of light?"

"Mack? Nah, not him. He's literally earth-bound. A Watcher. That's why you can't really see his wings. His job is to keep an eye on us wretched mortals and report back. He's over there, right now, talking to one of the messengers, who will slide back on up to get his next orders."

She squinted and wrinkled her nose. "So, right over there, there's an escalator to Heaven? I don't see anything."

"Not yet, you don't. We need to cross the circle. Follow and stay low."

They hunched down and skulked closer.

"And angels are just sliding up and down and delivering heaps of divine information?" She lost the wondrous expression and lowered her brows. "That sounds very much like interference, doesn't it?"

"Hey, now. I didn't bring you here to cause trouble. Just—try not to antagonize him, will yeh? He's usually a bit rammy after one of those things. I think it hurts him, you know, being stuck down here like some common mortal. He's obedient to the Will…but he misses home."

"You mean…" Chiara grasped his arm, half-turning him toward her. "He doesn't want to be here?"

"He's a Watcher. This is his deployment." He shrugged. "Trouble is, it's not a simple 18-month tour of duty and there's no leave. I always thought it sounded like a prison sentence but I try not to make him feel worse than he does. It's his place to be here. It's his duty. Who am I to judge or to criticize? It's the Will of God. I'm just a puny mortal, a pawn in this great and terrible game."

They crept toward the swatch of sunlight in the field. No ordinary sunlight…the grass glittered with life, the air held fragrances usually sullied by traffic and pollution. Birds were drawn to the area, filling the air with their songs. Even the wildlife seemed to congregate in the area. All was a sense of peace and serenity.

The air rippled around them, similar to the wards he'd placed around his vehicle. An invisible line. This one took a hell of a lot more than burning chicory.

Once they crossed the border into the sunlit space, that serenity vanished. It went from a pastoral picture to the trading floor on Wall Street, the inside of a war room on high alert.

Urgency was a flavor on the tongue as Simon pulled in the first lungful of tight, charged air. The atmosphere had become a buzz of voices and motion. Watchers, dozens of them with their stunted ghostly wings, gathered around the base of the Ladder, calling with hands cupped around their mouths, shouting and greeting the travelers.

The travelers didn't gracefully float up and down the ethereal ladder—they shot like they were rocket-launched, speed making them a golden blur. When they got to the bottom, they hovered over the ground to communicate with the Watchers, never touching the wretched earth, held aloft by the spread of their wings—

Oh, their wings. Simon rubbed his mouth, trying to hide his expression from Chiara. It was impossible to not be affected by a sight like that. The sight of an angel's wings made mortality seem like a petty, crude thing. All a man's concerns and triumphs and tragedies crumbled to mere nothings when faced with that breathtaking sight.

It stole a piece of a man's soul, seeing those angels. Definitive proof that God exists. It destroyed the very essence of faith. No longer can a man *believe* there is a God; no longer can he choose to do the right thing, the good thing, in the hopes that he will secure a place in Heaven. No longer does the concept of free will even exist.

Seeing angels, seeing the proof—it dropped like stones in a garden path, no twists, no turns, no forks in the road. Just a predetermined measure of steps that go from where a man currently stood to the feet of an unavoidable judgment.

Knowledge and belief were two totally different things. The main difference was the absence of the most vital nutrient a soul received: hope.

Simon and Chiara spent many long moments watching the angels. Eventually, the clouds shifted and the light shrank upwards, the Ladder dissipating. The Watchers each zapped out of sight, winking out, leaving no sign that they'd even been there.

Sound returned, too, normal waves of breeze and birdsong and traffic from the highway farther off.

"Well, that's it for tonight's episode, folks." Simon pushed to his feet, brushing the grass from his pants. "Thanks for your patronage and we look forward to you joining us again next week when we present another episode of The Celestial Prophesy show."

A crunch on gravel behind them made them both spin. Mack stood serenely behind them, hands folded in front of his waist.

"Jesus, Mack. I hate when you do that."

The angel clucked his tongue at the blasphemy. "I have a message."

"I figured as much. Well. Go on with it."

Mack remained silent, shifted his gaze toward Chiara.

"Oh, what? Her?" Simon scoffed. "Anything you have to say to me you can say in front of her."

"That's not how this works."

Simon heaved an exasperated sigh. "Sorry, kid. Mack here is shy in front of girls. They make him nervous, if you know what I mean."

"And that isn't what he means," Mack intoned.

Chiara raised her hands. "Hey. No worries. I'll just be over there, admiring the view of—actually, I'm not sure what that is."

"A gopher hole, from the looks of it. Enjoy." Simon watched her walk out of earshot before swinging a pissy look at Mack. "Satisfied?"

"Not my rules."

"Yeah, yeah." He took a tissue out of his pocket, ripped it in half, and wadded it, stuffing it into his ears. "Try to leave me in one piece this time, 'kay?"

Mack closed his eyes a moment.

When he opened them again, the pupils were gone, lost in a uniform metallic sheen. They glowed a magnificent brightness, like gold in the sun, just this side of painfully bright.

That was a beautiful thing. Always was. There was never a time that Simon took a message that he wasn't left feeling scoured and scrubbed by a gentle holy hand. It was like the sun shone only upon him, that he alone was worthy of the warmth. He'd never actually admit it, but it was a brief return to complete innocence, of being utterly worthy of the Creator's attention.

But, as with everything, there was a downside. The racket.

Mack's mouth opened impossibly wide, a veritable megaphone, the herald of God. The brightness streamed forth from his lips, that same golden glow. A cacophony of trumpets sounded in a blast that was not exactly meant for mortal eardrums.

The voice that thundered from Mack's unmoving lips was not his voice.

"*Light's scion, tarnished…Love's betrayer…A crushing blow will deliver to the lone-heart, the mortal savior of souls.*"

The light and the voice faded and Mack closed his mouth and eyes, falling in on himself a little before regaining his posture. It was the only time Simon ever saw a weakness in him. When he opened his eyes again, he was himself.

Simon squinted, pulling the tissue out wiggling his pinkie finger into his ear to soothe it. "Really, Mack? Another riddle?"

"Don't shoot the messenger, Simon. Metatron follows time-honored traditions."

"He also thinks I'm hard-of-hearing." He rolled the tissues between his palms and stuffed the wad into his pocket. "And a poet, too, apparently. Does he think I can interpret sonnets? Or that I even want to?"

Mack grabbed Simon's shoulder as he tried to turn away. "Don't be foolish. This message came high priority for your ears only. You were meant to know this. You are expected to stop this."

"It can mean anything, anyone. You know what I think it means? The Metatron gets a real charge out of delivering vagueness."

"I watched your face as you took the message." Mack took a step toward him, his face alight with eager empathy. "I saw your expression. What does your gut say?"

"You think it's me." He took a step back and rubbed his mouth. "Nah. Too poetic to be me. The lone-heart? Savior of souls?"

"You're a terrible liar. You resonated with the message. It's all in your eyes."

"Which reminds me," Simon said. "I need a new pair of shades. I'm still seeing Metatron retina burn."

"Do the right thing, Simon. Please. And...be careful."

"When aren't I?"

"I have to answer that?"

"Yeah, yeah. Off with you."

Mack turned as if he might walk away. The ghost of his wings thickened around him in a velveteen fog and he vanished with it.

Simon wished he could do the same. Just poof, vanish, bye-bye, leave a problem behind. Not that he could ever believe that prophesy was about Chiara...but nothing Mack had relayed in the past wasn't personal. Every pronouncement had somehow involved him.

Light's scion, tarnished...Love's betrayer...A crushing blow will deliver to the lone-heart, the mortal savior of souls...

Shaking his head, he turned back to look for Chiara. He'd figure this without dragging her into it.

This time, the Light was mistaken.

Had to be.

She'd watched from a discreet distance while Mack relayed his message, the angel's back toward her. She'd seen the light that bathed Simon's upturned face, his wondrous expression.

Kind of sweet, actually. It made her grin. Simon thought he was a true tough guy, the renegade magician who could pound his chest and make the demons run.

Standing vulnerable in front of an angel, receiving a divine message, his swagger was gone, his entire demeanor child-like in its innocence. Very unlike him, and yes. Very sweet.

When the glow faded, he once more donned the usual mantle of his pushed down eyebrows, the skeptical frown he wore most of the time. When he wasn't being a smart mouth.

She waited until the angel took his leave, disappearing behind the fog of his wings, before she made her way back over to Simon. He lit a cigarette while she scanned the field in the direction she'd seen Mack leave, making sure he truly was gone. "Did he have news?"

"He always does. Trick is figuring out which piece of news is actually news worthy." He swept a hand toward the trees, leaving a thin wavering ribbon of smoke to hang in the air. Together, they retraced their steps back through the woods, albeit at a less-breakneck speed.

She ducked under a branch he'd lifted for her. "Aren't you afraid you're being manipulated?"

"By that angel? Pshaw. You have to be kidding. That was the voice of the Metatron. The message is sort of a celestial recording. It's virtually tamperproof. You've never seen an angel play messenger?"

She resisted making a disapproving noise and turned her head, not wanting him to see her expression. "God and I aren't on speaking terms."

"Well, actually nobody is on speaking terms with Him, for that matter. But, seriously. When Mack says he has a message to deliver, I never doubt it's the real deal." The trees thinned and they emerged from the woods onto an empty road. His van was nowhere to be seen. He scratched his head and looked both ways before striking off to the right. "Might be a load of cryptic archaic horseshit sometimes, but it's not *his* horseshit. It's straight from the mouthpiece of the Almighty."

A car approached from the other direction. As nonchalant as he tried to be, he followed it with his hawk-sharp eyes. Once it had passed out of sight, he raised a hand. She stepped away, not wanting to get caught up in the edges of his magic.

He muttered a Latin phrase, breaking the ward and revealing the vehicle, still parked where they'd left it. He hadn't even bothered locking the doors.

She glared at him over the hood. "And it doesn't bother you that what he does is an act of war?"

He stared at her wordlessly before pulling open his door and climbing into the seat. When she slammed her door shut, it felt like a vacuum inside.

"War." He'd lost his saucy banter. "That's a heavy word."

"It's the only word." She fastened her seatbelt. "The Light versus the Dark, with only the razor edge of mortality between them. Those people—those lovely, ignorant people—they are all that keeps the war from spilling over and becoming a cataclysm. They are what keeps everything from being destroyed."

"Come on, you make it sound like Mack is trying to start the apocalypse."

She crossed her arms. She knew he had a close relationship with the angel, no matter how much he'd put Mack down. Simon talked a rebel's game but his loyalty to one side was unsettling. It was bias, not balance. "It's not the place of the divinities to interfere on Earth. Earth was created for mortals—and mortals alone."

"I don't get you. You correct demonic possessions. I'd say that's pretty much as anti-dark as a girl can get."

"Doesn't mean I approve of angels on Earth."

"But the Watchers—"

"Are divinities. You can't say they're only a step up from—" She faltered, searching for something that sounded Simon-esque. "Nosy gossipmongers."

He raised a finger and half-smiled, seeming to acknowledge the accuracy of her description. "He doesn't do anything—I dunno, angelic. I've never seen him sway a mortal or try to exert influence in any way."

Then he'd be the first, she thought. She'd had encounters with the angelic host before. Exerting influence seemed to be their stock in trade. "He doesn't influence you?"

"Not at all. He rats out demons, sure, and give me a nudge in the right direction, but it's up to me to do something about it. And in the end, we do the same thing, you and I. So, chill."

She grumbled. Not because she was angry but, rather, because deep down she wanted to believe him. "It's a principle."

"That's why I maintain relatively few principles to get hung up on." He started the van, turning the key twice until the engine caught.

No doubt of that. She chewed the corner of her lip. "Does he manifest to other mortals?"

"As far as I know, I'm the sole object of his charms."

That was more difficult to believe. "If I ever catch him trying to ride skin—"

He laughed. "That sounds ridiculously lewd coming from you."

She smirked and reached across to him, grabbing his collar. Effortlessly, she pulled him toward her until they were nose to nose, so close she could taste his breath. "I will exorcise him, and in case he doesn't know it, I will enjoy firstly explaining how very painful a process it is. And I will enjoy living up to my word."

He licked his lips and ducked his head. "Hope you don't have your heart set on it. I don't think that's something we'll have to worry about."

She released his jacket with a sullen tug. "Don't get me wrong—I don't hold anything against angels. I just don't like interference. The mortal world must be protected from outside influence. That's the privilege of being born mortal—to live securely in their own world. They deserve the ignorant bliss of never realizing there is a war that is scorching through the other planes."

"Yeah, well." He shrugged his jacket into place and shifted the van into gear. "I deserve that ignorant bliss, too. Guess it's just not my lot."

"Simon, I didn't mean—"

"I get it, okay? I get your point. But you know what?"

His knuckles paled under the force with which he gripped the steering wheel. "Life isn't fair, kid. And this is a tough game. I need every advantage I can get. You call it bias. I call it fighting to win. Maybe you want balance but I've seen the Dark and I will not let it win. I won't stop until it's gone."

She rolled her lips between her teeth. He was wrong in too many ways to count but this wasn't a good time to educate him to that particular end. Right now, his brows were bunched so low they almost touched. He was upset.

His position on the topic was merely a matter of vantage point. Better to wait until the conversation could be less emotional.

They drove back to Baltimore in pensive silence, the miles and the thoughts seeming to stretch on endlessly. She'd never given his "lot" much thought, beyond the obvious. His exterior, his actions and words, spoke clearly enough.

Or did they? Was it all a veneer? Was there something behind the swagger, the flash and the magic? Something she hadn't noticed?

Or had cared enough to seek?

One thing she knew—he wasn't in the mood for more discussion. The lines around his eyes seemed deeper, his posture weary against the back of the seat. Talking now wouldn't bring them closer. It would only drive him deeper into himself.

Back in town, he pulled up to the curb in front of her building but left the van running.

"You're not going in?" She couldn't keep dismay from tinting her voice. "Where will you go?"

"Eh," he said. "I've got to find some place to park this bus. Preferably some where they don't do street cleaning. I can't ward against getting smashed by a truck."

"You could try paid parking, you know."

"That's an idea." He grinned, as if already deciding upon a devilish alternative. "I'll see you later."

Maybe sooner, rather than later, she thought, watching as he drove away.

He slipped into traffic and headed back uptown. He was thinking…Fell's Point. More bars per square mile than anywhere else in the US, if he recalled correctly. It had become more or less tradition to head there following a Ladder, when he needed a little bit of sense-dulling after an encounter with the Metatron.

He pinioned the steering wheel with his knees and tugged a piece of chicory out of his cigarette pack, looking for an empty space at the curb. Pausing over, he burned the stick and cast the charm, waiting for a break in the traffic before pulling out again and heading to the marina. The parking lot by the waterfront was clearly marked with a big sign that read *Monthly Parking by Permit Only*.

Tonight, he gave himself permission to park there. He gently eased the now-invisible van past the attendant's booth, waving to the kid who perched on his seat inside, intent on his phone. Kid never even looked up, despite the loose fan belt that squealed a bit. The van was invisible, but not silent.

He took a spot at the furthest end. "Paid parking," he said, partly to himself. "Good idea, kid."

A few things first…

A rub of intention oil between thumb and finger made drawing the window curtains a snap—literally. The center console contained a deck of worn playing cards, which he flipped through, one by one, until he found the one he wanted: a card that, amazingly, looked exactly like the parking placards this lot used. With a chortle, he hung it from the rearview before getting out.

He made sure every door was locked, and added a GO AWAY ward before cancelling the invisibility spell. The last thing he needed was someone thinking the spot was empty and trying to park on top of him.

Taking a deep breath of wind-swept air, admiring the play of lights upon the early twilight-sheened harbor, he nodded to himself as he pocketed his keys and set off in search of dinner. Wouldn't be hard. This was one of his favorite neighborhoods. Plenty of places to take a load off.

And plenty of ghosts, too, he remembered a short time later, as he waited for the waitress to come back with a lager and a menu. He noticed the girl sitting in the booth across, the table covered with bins of silverware and stacks of napkins. Apparently the waitresses used this as a prep station.

So it was a little odd for a pretty honey-blonde, mid-twenties, maybe, to be sitting there.

Then he noticed she was a bit transparent. Not so odd, then. Hauntings were as commonplace as cobblestone around here.

She seemed to watch the comings and goings but never got up, never spoke, never interacted. He watched her with intense curiosity. Every ghost was like a movie: a visual with a story. Sometimes the stories were dull. Sometimes, not so dull. It was the reason he'd sewn a braid of sweet grass into the lining of his jacket.

Never easy to tell right off if a ghost was a residual or an intelligent haunting. Over the years, he'd learned that the best implement for investigation was a simple, inexpensive one: good manners.

He lifted his glass to the girl and smiled. "Cheers."

"You can see me?" Her voice was drafty and hollow

with a little bit of a pre-echo to each word.

Yep, definitely a ghost. And no, not residual. "Sure, I can. Everything okay, miss?"

She shook her head. "I...I'm not sure. I've been sitting here forever and no one has even asked if I wanted to order."

"They seem super busy tonight. I'm sure someone will be along for you."

"I was on a blind date," she said. "He seemed okay but something...came over him. He..."

"Did he hurt you?"

"I don't remember. We were standing outside this window. I just remember him kissing me one minute—it wasn't slutty, it was just a cheek thing."

He lifted his hands, palms out. "Not judging."

"And the next thing I knew, he just—pushed me. Everything was cold and I fell over and here I was. How did I fall through the wall? It doesn't make sense. Because I was still standing outside the window." Her eyes big and confused, she reached out to him, pleading. "Why was I still out there?"

She peered at him, leaning over toward him. "It's still here. Why are you still here?"

Before he could answer, one of the servers slid into the booth and started to wrap bundles of cutlery. The ghost wisped away into nothingness.

"Huh." He took a long drought. "Hope you find your answers, sweetheart."

"I'm sorry?" The waitress looked at him. "Did you say something?"

He pointed to the far side of his head. "Earpiece. Phone call. Sorry."

The crab cakes were spectacular, as usual. This place

didn't gunk them up with an over-abundance of filler. While he ate, he let the Metatron's last message roll through his mind, over and over, as he tried to break it apart and interpret each section.

Light's scion, tarnished. Okay, a child of the light. Could mean any number of things. First off, a follower, a believer—which only narrowed it down to just about two billion people, and that was only counting Christians. Lots of people believed in God. God just didn't look the same to all of them.

Okay, so a believer being light's scion in this case would be a little too vague. The Metatron was many things but he wasn't trite.

So it had to refer to an actual child who'd been born to one of the Light, with a capital L. That definitely narrowed the playing field.

Could be someone of the Christ line, the Merovingians and their innumerable secret offshoots. Trouble with that would be in calling the entire family "born of the Light." Divine DNA could travel only so far before becoming dilute to the point of impotency. Pretty much just science.

Or...He caught the waitress' eye and signaled with his glass for a refill. It could be one descended from angels. Angel blood did not dilute, no matter how hard one tried. Christ was unique and wholly human. Angels were definitely not.

And they loved getting a little action. The Watchers, who didn't have wings, could pass for regular human—and sane, if they kept their mouths shut long enough.

His stomach flopped. He didn't personally know too many angels and Mack didn't strike him as a baby daddy. But Enochians—he could name one or two of those.

Dammit. He closed his eyes and massaged his brows with his thumbs. Chiara.

He pushed around the last of his Old Bay fries, scowling. There had to be another angle, another piece he wasn't seeing. Another clue he hadn't found yet. No reason why it had to keep coming back to her.

"Hope you don't mind if I wait for your check. Had three skip out on me this month." The waitress put down his beer and the bill. "This beer's not on there. Girl at the bar sent it."

"Who?"

She shrugged and waited while he pulled out his wallet. "Redhead. You'll know her when you see her."

He waved her away when she offered change. "Thanks for the tip."

"Thanks for yours." She winked and held up the bills. "Have a good time."

"Maybe I will."

The waitress cleared his plates. Oh, crap. He breathed into his cupped hand and sniffed. Did he have crab breath? A quick mental inventory of the herbs he carried came up empty on the pleasing fragrance scale. Dammit again. He knew he should have refilled the fennel compartment of his weekly pill organizer.

Hey, things like that came in handy and they fit into an inside pocket. Practical magic was the best magic.

With a sigh that said things were pretty much as good as they were going to get, he slid out of the booth and took a swig of beer, swishing it around his mouth before grabbing his jacket and strolling through the dining room to the bar.

He scanned the row of stools. At the far end, one face turned in his direction, a woman who dipped her chin to hide a quick smile when they made eye-contact. Her heart-shaped face framed by soft waves of shoulder-length auburn hair, she wore an off-the-shoulder slouchy sweater.

Very pretty. And definitely looking at him again.

C'mon, Simon. You face down the minions of the netherworld without blinking an eye. Why's that girl got you frozen in your tracks?

He gave himself a mental shove forward. Fortune favored the bold, right?

"You didn't sneak out the back door," she said with a hopeful smile when he took the seat next to her. She had to raise her voice to be heard over the clamor of the crowded bar area. "That's a good sign."

"You didn't have horns." He set down his beer and leaned an elbow on the bar, sitting sideways to face her. Near-empty martini glass on a napkin in front of her. Sweater on her lap. Cross-body purse securely in front. No ring on her left hand. *Stop the surveillance, Simon.* "I figured it was a good way to start."

"Wow." She wrinkled her nose and laughed, a bit weakly. "Dark sense of humor."

"Wasn't kidding, but that's okay. Thanks, by the way." He lifted his glass in a mock toast. "What's your name?"

"Mimi." She toyed with a lock of hair, twirling it on her fingers, and nibbled her bottom lip. "You are?"

"Kevin." The lie slid out so much easier that it should have. Oh, well. It wasn't like he normally ran about yelling his true name. Honestly, the only ones who used it these days were Chiara and Mack. Everyone else who knew it was either dead or in hell.

Hopefully, this new acquaintance wouldn't end up as either.

"Nice to meet you, Kevin." She held out her hand for a shake, her smile innocent.

Ah, okay. She wanted to shake hands. Could be…manners. Could be luring him into a shady deal. He'd already accepted a beer. What if the handshake was a contract?

A surreptitious glance around him revealed no one was burning a black candle or chanting from the darkened depths of a sinister-looking hood. Or even paying attention, really.

Her smile faltered, her outstretched hand dipping. He was being rude.

He took her hand, gingerly, and exhaled hard when he made contact with actual flesh. Not a ghost, at least. What a relief. He had started to think human girls had given up on him.

But no handshake. He kissed the back of her hand like a gentleman, hoping to close the deficit of his awkward behavior. "So, ah, Mimi. You make a habit out of sending drinks to strange men?"

"Not really," she admitted. Her face flushed in a pretty glow after the kiss-the-hand move. "I wasn't even sure it would work."

"It worked. I'm here." His smile faded after a moment. Wherever he went, trouble was rarely less than a stone's throw away. "You look like a nice girl and everything, but..."

"I do?" Her brow creased and she pouted, crestfallen but for a humorous twinkle in her eye. "I was going for something more like...Irresistible Bombshell. Or at the very least, Definitely Worth Walking Home."

It was becoming very hard to not enjoy this.

"Is that how it's done these days? Labelling? I shudder to think what my label would read." He toyed with the glass, running his finger around the rim. "Perhaps Approaching Expiration Date."

"You're not that old," she protested.

"Looks can deceive."

"Well, what I see is...a nicely dressed man who looks at

a girl's face when she talks and who obviously has good taste in food."

He narrowed his eyes. She knew this…how?

"I asked your waitress. The crab cakes really are the bomb. But I wasn't watching you eat, or anything. I noticed you when I walked to the ladies' room." She brushed her hair back from her forehead and frowned. "I told you I'm not good at this, didn't I?"

He rested his elbows on the bar, letting her chatter away. This was nice. This banter. This small talk with a charming woman. No threat of damnation or having to listen to Mack lecturing about why he needed to get away from her. Just in case…he swept the room with a quick gaze. Nope. No Mack. "And I looked lonely, huh? Is this a pity drink?"

"No, not lonely. Just alone. And you're much too attractive to be sitting some place alone." Suddenly, her eyes flew open wide and she covered her mouth. "Oh, gosh. Did I just say that?"

"Yes, you did." he said, laughing. "Who even says 'gosh' anymore?"

"I know, right? Certainly not someone who bares her shoulder like it's 1986 and impulsively buys a drink for a guy just because she watched him eat dinner and imagined what he'd look like without a shirt on." She nodded, lifting her shoulders in an elegant shrug. "So, Kevin, what's the verdict?"

"Hmm?"

"Maybe…definitely worth walking home?" She half-smiled and flipped her hair a little, hope in her eyes. Definitely new to the singles game.

No worries. He was out of practice, himself. But that was the best part of the game, wasn't it? The practice? Fortunate to have come across someone who was, to all appearances, a very good sport.

And he was never one to turn down a good time.

"I think…it's a lovely night for a walk." He stood, held out a hand to help her down off her stool. "Can I take you home?"

She slipped her hand into his and led him out the door.

The sun had gone down some time ago, and the relentless harbor breeze had developed teeth. Despite her sweater, Mimi shuddered, nearly stumbling.

"You okay?" He grabbed her arm, afraid she would go face first into the sidewalk.

"Fine," she answered. "Never better."

The address she gave him was close by. He knew this neighborhood well enough that he could envision not only exactly where her apartment building stood but also its relative proximity to local ley lines and churches. Fairly inactive spot, although still lousy with ghost walk touring companies. At least he wasn't walking into a paranormal war zone.

She wound her arms though his, snuggling against him as they strolled along the sidewalk, weaving through the stream of nightlife. After a block or two, she pointed toward a side street, away from the waterfront.

"Shortcut," she said.

It wasn't. That much he knew. He gazed beyond her pointing finger and surveyed the alley. The streetlights didn't reach very deep between the buildings. He wasn't afraid of the dark. Neither, it seemed, was she. Funny. He hadn't gotten that impression in the bar.

He peered in, seeing very little of what lay down the lane. "You always charge down creepy dark Baltimore streets?"

"Trust me. This is safer." She drifted to a stop and backed into the shadows, drawing him with her. With a smile, she slipped her hands up his chest, looping her fingers around his neck. "And quieter. There's a dog about a block and a half up that way."

"I don't mind dogs," he said, and immediately wanted to kick himself. Boy. Really out of practice.

"Would you mind this?" She closed what little distance remained between them and went up on her toes, pulling his face down to hers.

A girl with a plan. He liked that.

He circled her with his arms, pulling her closer. A plan *and* curves. And soft lips. *Thank you, Luck,* he thought. *Definitely a lady tonight.*

And hot. Definitely hot. He faltered, breaking the kiss. This girl was overheating.

She reclaimed his lips but this time he broke away forcefully. Gripping her arms, he held her still, trying not to hurt her. "You okay? You were freezing just a few minutes ago. You don't have a fever or something, do you?"

"I'm burning for you," she said, the indirect light from the street glinting off her open smile. "Come on, Kevin."

Her voice slipped deeper and she twisted her forearms around his, breaking his hold, sliding her hands around his waist, snuggling closer. "Don't go all cold on me now."

She kissed him again, tugging up the bottom of his t-shirt and sliding her fingertips along his back, around his sides, up his chest. "Mmm. Feels just like how I imagined you'd look."

When she brushed her palm against his amulet she hissed and snatched her hands back. Her eyes glowed, pulsing red. "Wretched, wretched trinket!"

"Oh, you gotta be kidding me." Dammit. A real she-devil. He rubbed his mouth, trying to wipe away the remnants of her kiss. "And here I thought we had a real connection."

Of course not. That would be too easy. He felt through his pocket for his St. Bridget's cross.

"I hate exorcism on a full stomach," he said. "You have to wait an hour after eating or you'll get cramps. Or was that swimming? Anyway." He thrust the cross up between them, pinning her to the wall. The host twisted her face away, steam rising from her shoulders, struggling like a fly on a glue trap. Holding the cross in his teeth, he pulled out his thumb rings and slid them on before taking the cross in hand again "Had a great time, sweetheart, but too much of a good thing is bad for you."

SO IS THIS. The demon snarled and focused its sullen red stare on the cross.

Wait. It could look upon a blessed object? Not a good sign.

Neither was the smoke that started to leak from the cross.

The relic burst into flame and he dropped it, fanning his fingers. Bad, bad stuff. With a single clap of his hands, he stretched the stream of power between the rings.

THAT WON'T BE ENOUGH TO PROTECT YOU FROM ME.

"That's why I'm here," Chiara announced from behind him.

Chiara? When did she get here? For some reason, he wasn't surprised. He didn't take his eyes off the demon.

No longer held in place, the host stood before the wall, arms bunched, looking like a pro-wrestler, ready to jump off the top rope. Damn shame. He'd liked the taste of her lip gloss.

"Two exorcists, one demon." He clucked his tongue. "You really need to be careful who you try picking up in a bar, sweetheart. Didn't someone teach you about stranger danger?"

He held up his hands, the arc of magic sizzling between his rings. The air tasted like a lightning storm.

"So much for a night off, huh." He glanced over his shoulder at Chiara. The light from his binding rings illuminated the alley, chasing back the shadows. That's what his magic did. It beat down the rising darkness.

"Stay back, kid." He reached for the demon, his smile jagged and humorless. "This one is mine."

The demon snarled, a shredding glimpse of sabre-sharp teeth, and swiped at the wall. Sparks scattered under the tips of its talons. Sullen streaks of light appeared, bleeding through the break in the bricks.

The heat that rushed out caused the arc of magic to sizzle out. His concentration was broken. That was all it took for the spell to falter.

He backed off in a hurry, pulling Chiara away with him. "Bitch can open portals. Get back, Chi—"

The demon pried the edges of the portal back and climbed through the gash. The tattered edges began sealing back up as the portal slowly closed in on itself.

Chiara turned to him, mouth open in protest.

"Aw, let it go," he said. "We need to regroup, rethink what we're up against."

"Oh, Simon." She wiped her mouth with the back of her hand and shifted her weight from one foot to the other. "When will you learn?"

She bolted headlong toward the wall, smashing through the nearly closed portal. The rippling edges melded back together and disappeared, leaving no more than ordinary wall.

No portal. No demon. No Chiara.

"Oh, hell." He lit a cigarette. "Women."

Stowing his lighter, he crossed his arms and leaned against the wall. Nothing to do but wait.

He didn't have to wait very long. A few moments later, the portal opened in a flash of eerie green light and a pair of people stumbled out. The jagged hole in the fabric of reality snapped shut with a muffled boom that made his eardrums bulge.

He checked his watch. "You know how to keep a guy waiting, don't you?"

The girl collapsed. All signs of demonic possession were gone.

So were signs of life.

Simon knelt over her and leaned close to her face. No breath against his cheek. The redhead's eyes were closed, her face slack with a terrible peace. Simon jammed two fingers on to the side of the girl's neck. No pulse. "She's not breathing."

Chiara wavered on her feet, looking more tired that he'd ever seen her. She dropped down to her knees, head too heavy to hold up. One look at her face and Simon knew he was on his own for this part.

He pinched the girl's nose closed and tilted her chin, giving her two breaths. The chest rose. He started compressions. What was the song they used to keep the rhythm? Staying Alive? What a stupid song.

Elbows locked, he gave compressions until his back started to ache, the lagging adrenaline leaving exhaustion in its wake. Two more rescue breaths.

The girl coughed.

Simon sat back on his heels and licked his lips. Watermelon. Things could have been so much fun tonight, if she's actually been in her right mind.

The host took a deep, shuddering breath just as the terror took hold. She scrambled back against the wall, looking like a psychotic monkey in a cage. Eyes close to popping out, she babbled like a madwoman. "Where—what was that screaming? Fire, fire everywhere—I was in hell! Oh, my god. Hell! Who are you?"

"Good Samaritan," Simon replied.

Chiara crawled over to anoint her. "G'won," she slurred. "Get out before it decides to fight to get you back."

The girl grabbed her hand and peered into Chiara's face, chin trembling. "Was I...dead?"

"Yeah. And that guy saved you. Another reason to leave. You owe him a favor now."

The redhead scrambled to her feet and lurched away, snatching glances of them over her shoulder.

"Next time you jump through a portal after a host, warn me. Mortals don't travel well the first time." He hunched down next to Chiara and hooked his hands under her arms to hoist her up. "You okay, kid?"

She gasped in pain.

"No. I'm really not." She took a shallow, whistling breath and turned her face toward him. Blood ran from her hairline, dripping down the right side of her face. "Get me home. Before—"

She pressed her hand to her waist. It came away dark and wet. She whimpered, a sound of pain and fear. She crumpled against him, her head drooping.

"Chiara?" He gently shook her. "Honey, wake up."

No response. She was limp and heavy in his hands. Home. She had to get home.

He hefted her and started running. At the end of the alley, he uttered a chant, trying to cloak them from passersby. Couldn't do the full spell without burning a stick of chicory and he couldn't do that carrying her.

At best, the spell would blur them, make them less noticeable. And right now all he could hope for was the best.

Getting her through the door was a challenge he didn't need. He chuffed out a charm that blew the door flat against the wall, the clatter ricocheting across the street. Adrenaline and sheer force of will propelled him up the stairs. He kicked the door open.

"Upstairs." Chiara's eyes fluttered. "The end of the hall."

Her shirt was crimson, sopping with blood. It slapped wetly against him when he moved. "You need a doctor."

"No. The pool."

He staggered up the staircase, unable to feel his legs. "You've lost too much blood. I don't think a swim is what you need."

Chiara gasped, each breath seeming to bring new pain. "It's the only thing."

He turned the corner and spied the door at the end of the hall. It swung open, smoothly and silently, as he rushed toward it. Once inside, he skidded to a stop, nearly dropping her.

He'd only glanced in here, briefly, the first night he stayed over. A marble bath, thirty foot ceilings, a glass tiled sunken bath. The water was milky, a blanket of steam snaking across its surface.

The décor had a mystical, murky feel to it, like oil on wind, and he struggled to remember what had ever made him consider spending time in here the last time he visited.

"Hurry," she whispered. "Get me in. Don't touch the water, don't touch."

"Dammit, what am I supposed to do? Just tell me!"

"Set me down. The edge."

He knelt and gently laid her at the water's edge. The grey pallor of her face made his heart pound even harder.

She looked up at him, grabbing his shirt. Their gazes locked. "Whatever you do—don't get wet."

He nodded wordlessly.

She rolled off the edge and sank out of sight. No bubbles, no splash. The water swallowed her like it was a pool of molten metal.

Simon screamed at the surface.

Nothing.

Nothing at all.

The surface stilled.

Time passed, but just how much time, he hadn't a clue. There was no sense of movement. His breaths barely stirred the air in front of his face. And, although initially it had taken many long, dragging moments, he eventually had detected a scent in here, subtle yet pervasive.

Was it the water? The steam slicking its way across the mirrored service? Or was it something that burned in the braziers glowing in the corners of the room? The incense was acrid, scraping his sinuses and throat, leaving rawness in its wake.

This was a terrible place to spend any time. Why someone would put a pool in a room that stank like a chemical fire—

Wait a minute, Simon, try using your pea brain a minute. She's not swimming, is she? She's lying on the bottom of a pool that doesn't have actual water in it, bleeding out from a devastating wound. If she's not dead, she soon will be. Should be.

He banged his head against the tiles. And there wasn't a goddamned thing he could do about it. She said *don't get wet* and the tone of her voice, even in pain, promised him she meant it. He took that part seriously.

He hunched against the wall, knees drawn to his chest. Various charms lay scattered about him, each one considered but discarded. There was no amulet that would be any use to her, not now.

Now, he sat motionless, staring with vacant eyes at the still surface, the steam rising in vague shapes that left him quietly terrified.

A soft sound from the pool roused him. Chiara slowly emerged, rising to the top, floating still and silent, face slack, eyes closed. The milky liquid streamed down her skin in thick rivulets.

Simon crept toward the edge, fear in his eyes.

"Chiara?" he whispered. "Are you—"

Her eyes snapped open and she sucked in a loud lungful of air. Panting, she looked wildly around like she didn't know where she was. But then she saw him. Her gaze locked on his face, she gradually calmed.

He remained perfectly still, unwilling to spook her.

Swallowing hard, she nodded, as if reassuring herself. She waded toward him, her breaths loud against the tiled walls, and draped her arms on the edge.

He drew back from the water that dripped from her skin, forming a small puddle beneath her arms.

She drooped her cheek onto the back of her hand.

"Chiara." His voice was ragged, the screaming and the dry acridity of the room roughening his speech. "What can I do?"

"I could use a shower." She smiled wanly. "Hand me a towel?"

Wrapped in thick towels, Chiara dozed on her crummy couch, her head on Simon's leg. He'd dragged it over to the grand fire place to help keep her warm. He stroked her damp hair, absent-mindedly, having an oddly peaceful moment.

Maybe he needed a bath, too. Her blood had run down his waist, soaking his pants, making him look like he'd been the one who was hurt. His clothes were still marred by dried, dark brown streaks that had stiffened as the blood dried. It made him itchy.

All this reminded him of past experiences. Back then, there'd been no magic pool. Those who had bled didn't survive. He'd been terrified that she wouldn't, either.

Now, she slept, her shoulders rising and falling with each breath. She was alive. And he never had felt more relieved in his entire life.

She stirred, slowly opening her eyes. She pushed herself upright and sat next to him, drawing her bare legs up onto the couch.

"Ah, there she is." Simon reached for a throw pillow and snugged it against her for support. "Feeling better after your tub?"

She laughed gently and ruffled her fingers through her hair. "Much."

"Let me have a look at that wound. I thought you would have bled out by now."

She leaned away and parted the towel enough for him to see her bare waist.

There was no wound. The skin was perfect.

Wow. Just—wow. He had not the words, for once. Simon whistled in astonishment. "No need for a reeking but mind-blowingly effective poultice, I see."

She re-secured the towel and tugged a fleece throw off the back of the couch. "I did say I was much better."

Better. Back from the dead was more like it. Simon snorted. "Angel magic, eh? I should have guessed."

She scooted away. The smile she wore was thin and bittersweet. "You would have guessed wrong."

Poor kid. Her dual nature truly tortured her, didn't it? The last thing she needed was to feel bad about circumstances beyond her control.

"Maybe," he said. "But I guess that's because I try to look on the bright side of things." He pulled a lofty face at her. "I am, above all things, an optimist."

"You?" She scoffed, the line of her mouth hinting at a wry smile. "An optimist?"

"Sure. I firmly believe that things will absolutely, positively, without doubt, go to utter and complete shit. But, but—" he continued, talking over her chuckling. "I also believe that all this can't be for nothing. There's a reason why I can do what I do, why Mack singled me out. Things will go to shit, over and over, but I'll just keep kicking it back at them. I'll fight. And I'll do it beside you because I absolutely believe in you."

Her expression lost some of the weight it had been carrying. "I've always done this alone."

"You're not alone. Not as long as I'm around."

"Yeah." She patted his leg. "Too bad you couldn't be here forever."

"Not going anywhere at the moment. I kind of forgot my van."

"Not what I meant, but still." She reached for his hand. "Thank you."

"Where did that portal go?" Simon leaned over for his pack of cigs. "Kid was in rougher shape than you were when you came back through."

"Considering she was dead…"

"Nah, just knocked out. Portal travel makes you dizzy and nauseous and feeling like someone gave you an atomic wedgie but instead of using your underwear, it's your stomach—"

"Wasn't a portal." She cut him off. "It was a hell gate.

And she went to hell. And she came back dead."

Simon sat unmoving, agape. It was impossible.

"No." His voice was perfectly reasonable, but his brain was a clanking jumble of thoughts that just didn't fit together. "Hell gates can't open here."

"They can. And they do." She sighed. "And that's a huge problem."

Hell gates were a problem, all right.

Simon had studied them under one of his masters, an eccentric Cambridge scholar named Kent who claimed he'd stayed in Aleister Crowley's dormitory and had been visited several times by the old magician's ghost.

Admittedly, it was the wild name-dropping that had led Simon to the old gent, begging him to take him on, but the hell gate thing had come clean out of the blue. One night of expounding on the subject had secured Simon's devotion to his master and put Crowley out of his head altogether.

But hell gates were not permitted on the mortal plane. That had been the big take away from those three years of apprenticeship.

(It had taken Simon nearly twice that long to discover where Master Kent had later hidden his apprenticeship blood amulet, the one that kept him firmly in servitude to his master. Mages were annoyingly jealous of rank and seniority and often went through ridiculous lengths to keep from being turned on by their former students. And Kent hadn't even really been an overly jealous sort of person.)

The years thinned a bit, and Simon couldn't help but remember those days and nights he'd spent with Kent. Back then, Simon was still wet behind the ears. Just come off a two-year apprenticeship with an exorcist priest. The Crowley thing was a much-needed distraction. Two years of pulling demons out of people tended to leave a guy's spirit a little bruised.

"Why can't they be opened?"

Simon had been sitting on a cabinet in Kent's study, drinking a cheap beer, having a cheap smoke. Then again, cheap was pretty much all an out-of-work twenty-six-year old could afford.

Kent sat near his fireplace, bathed in the warm ruddy glow, swirling the dregs of a tumbler of Scotch. The fine cigar would be next. It was how they decompressed after a long afternoon of circle spells and grimoire memorization.

Tradition. For Kent, tradition wasn't habit. It was the structure that kept his life and his world and the whole of civilization from tumbling into powdery ruins.

Kent had made another of his vague references to hell gates, the kind he never followed up with an explanation. A slip up, a sign that he was exhausted enough to let his guard down. Usually, Simon was also too tired to pursue the thread.

This night, Simon wasn't worn out to the bones. His tolerance was developing. He wasn't done training. He wanted to know more.

Always more.

Kent did that to him. He gave him a hunger to learn. Damn professors and their educational hoodoo.

The older man, jowls bunching against his collar, frowned into his near-empty glass. "Because a demon has to do it. And demons cannot walk on this plane."

"Why not?" Simon didn't add *Because angels sure do.*

"People get possessed all the fricken time."

"But those are possessions. Demon entities spiritually manifesting in a mortal body. Basically, really bad ghosts."

"Demons can be summoned. They can come out of hell and do real shit."

"No." Kent's tone was resolute, the sound of a centuries-old conviction. "They can't."

Simon scowled behind his bottle as he drained the last of his lousy beer. How could he argue without revealing his worst crime? Say, *I summoned a demon when I was seventeen? Had it kill an asshole from my school? Watched it drag a little girl screaming into hell?*

That's a quick way to get expelled.

"There are rules, Alliant. Rules of heaven and rules of hell. I will admit that here in between the rules get a bit...muddied." No mistaking that twinkle in his eye. He might look like a dignified old chap but he'd been a literal hell raiser in his gone-by. "But the rules still hold. No angels or demons upon the earth."

"And rules can't be broken?"

"They should never be broken."

Should. That was nothing more than a theoretical word. "But portals," Simon persisted. "Those are possible."

"Yes. Magical travel from one place to another has been a long-standing practice. England has a rich history of magical practice, you see..."

Here went the speech. Simon knew it by heart and recited in his head, lock-step with Kent.

"...a history that can be traced back to the days when Arthurian legends were still being written. England was magic, still is even today. But today it is a secret practice. To practice out in the open would lead to hysteria. Mayhem. Murder."

"Yeah, yeah. Evidence of which is ample in our own

history in New England, just a few miles from here. The Salem witch hunts were a tragedy that never should have been allowed to happen." Simon rubbed his forehead. "But portals can be opened."

"Of course."

"Then why not hell gates?"

"Because a man is not a demon, even when he's possessed." Kent eyed him over the tops of his glasses. "You're an exorcist. You should know that."

"Yeah. It left me with this annoying sense of value for human life."

"No one is perfect," Kent said, his voice lilting with mild amusement.

"Says the man who was intimate with Crowley's ghost."

"Please. Do not use the words *intimate* and *Crowley* in the same sentence. He had a reputation, you know. Even someone of my own nefarious past has no wish to be equated with Crowley's—"

Simon cut him off with a laugh. "You? A nefarious past?"

"I'll have you know I was part of HRM's Special Forces. We were quite active during the Second World War. I may or may not have been charged with the solemn task of dealing with Hitler."

"Hitler?" Simon nearly fell off his perch. "Are you kidding me?"

"Hitler was a fanatical occultist. He had a library full of grimoires."

"You're avoiding—"

"I'm informing. That is my role as master, is it not? Now. Where was I? Oh, yes. England wasn't the only country with a history of magic. But magic is shaped with the intent of the practitioner. Hitler was obsessed with demons. It was said he summoned Molloch."

"Do you believe it?"

"Rubbish. But Hitler believed it. He quoted from Schertel at great length. *He who does not have the demonic seed within himself will never give birth to a magical world.* Metaphorical, of course. 'Demonic seed' was a clever way of describing ruthless ambition."

"Are you sure about that?"

"I have to be." Kent shoved himself up to his weary feet and plodded over to the cabinet where his humidor was stored. There would be no further discussion once the cigar was lit. Tradition. "It's what keeps me sane…"

∞

Simon sat in a strange bar. He'd been trying out new places since his last haunt went up in demon smoke. While the jukebox was appropriately loaded with Pearl Jam and Stone Temple Pilots and the like, it lacked a certain *je ne sais quoi.* He sniffed, deeply. That was it. The air.

Too clean in here.

He swirled his glass, letting the last of his trip down memory lane wash away. Kent. Hell gates. Simon thought about that particular conversation more often than he'd liked. It wasn't because he was comforted by it.

Oh, no. Just the opposite.

It made him wince, a physical knee-jerk reaction to a shame that never lost its freshness.

"You are troubled."

Startled out of his reverie, Simon looked up to see Mack, perched on a bar stool next to him.

"Nah." Simon tipped his glass and drained the last of the whiskey. "Just thinking."

"About?"

How to describe Kent? Certainly no single word was encompassing enough. Professor. Mage. Master. Legend.

The whiskey was working today, poisoning him with

sentiment. Maybe one word would come close. And close was enough for now. "An old friend."

"His memory causes you pain?"

Simon swung a heavy look at the angel. "Can I ask you a question?"

Mack nodded one, slowly. "You may."

"But it doesn't mean you'll answer. I get it. Anyway." He drew a deep breath. "Is it true that demons cannot walk on our plane?"

"Odd question. You are a demonologist. Are you doubting their existence?"

"No. But I'm thinking about something an old master once told me. He said there are rules. He said that neither angels nor demons can walk upon the mortal plane."

Mack bowed his head. "Your master is correct."

"But you're an angel."

"I am a Watcher now."

"Still, an angel."

"In name only. Have you ever seen my wings?" Mack spun his stool a quarter turn to face him. The angel's face was stretched into plaintive lines. "It's because I no longer have them. They collected my wings when I began my service. It is the way of things. Angels may not tread upon the earth as long as mortals live."

"I don't understand—"

"You are not permitted to understand." Mack shook head, wearing a look of resignation, and heaved a sigh. "Some things you must accept."

"Then if you're not an angel anymore, what are you?"

"I am..." Mack turned back to the bar, his gaze lowered. "Blessed."

By this time, the whiskey had also done its other job—killing his patience. Simon popped his palm on the bar top. "Mortal?"

"No."

"So I can't kill you?"

Mack shrugged, a very human gesture. "You could try."

"Can I bind you?"

"If I were into such things." The barest hint of a smile tilted his mouth. "I had no idea that *you* were."

"Quit it, jackass. I'm talking magic."

"Quite impervious, thank you." Mack tilted his head and peered at Simon. "You are still troubled."

"What do you know about hell gates?"

Mack's phantom wing fog arced out before tucking back, tightly, like the flex and clench of a new fist. The air tasted like tin.

Whoops. Trigger word. *Ho, ho, now the birdcage had been rattled. Someone's feathers just got ruffled.*

Mack turned his head, his jaw bunching as he bit off each word. "I do not know of what you speak."

"Bullshit, Mack. Look, you just spilled the holy mystery of why I only see the ghost of angel's wings on you. That's pretty big stuff. This is infinitely smaller but monumentally important to me. Can hell gates be opened here? On this plane?"

Mack looked rather uncomfortable discussing it. "Aye, if a demon were to do it. But demons are not permitted to walk upon this plane. Thus it is a moot point."

"Is it, really?"

Mack looked away. "I am sorry you are troubled by your memories, Simon. I will pray for you to find peace."

Simon slammed the glass down, making a guy across the bar jump and fumble his bottle, spilling beer across the bar. The bartender shot a reproachful look at Simon, who just waved him on with an impatient gesture. *Get him another beer on me. Get him ten. I don't care.*

"You do that." Simon gritted his teeth. "You go pray

somewhere. In the meantime, I'll just *do*. I'll do without waiting for a favor or help from a divine hand. I'll roll up my sleeves and put on my boots because there is a ton of shit for me to do out there, even without you giving me the extra-credit work."

It was the truth. He sensed trouble, even now. Felt it like a storm coming, a change in the air pressure. If there were horses nearby, they'd be restless or something. Whatever. He didn't need horses to tell him someone was out there that needed doing.

He glared back at Mack but his angry resolution faltered a little once he saw him. Mack had gone strangely still.

Simon eyed him. No longer sitting with elbows on the rail, Mack had gone all tall and statuesque, his odd eyes gleaming. On angel alert. Whatever trouble Simon had sensed, Mack had sensed it, too.

"Well, I'm gonna head." Simon leaned back and dug into his front pocket for his money. Time to settle the tab and start another one somewhere else. "No sense sitting here drinking by myself."

"You should stay here." Mack raised a palm, his voice weirdly hollow. "I believe there is a Ladder forming. You will wait here for my return."

A slight warming in the center of Simon's chest made him rub it. Funny. The itchy spot was right under his amulet.

Which meant, it had just expended power to protect him.

And if it just expended power to protect him, then it meant someone just tried to use magic on him.

And Mack had just commanded him to wait here.

Hmm.

Mack had never spelled him before. Simon never even thought that he could.

Or suspected that he would.

He measured each breath, forcing himself to appear relaxed. *Poker face, Simon. Something big just happened and he doesn't want you to know.*

Poker face was easy. After all, it was just his regular expression. Those thick Irish eyebrows came in handy sometimes. Wouldn't be the first time someone tried to force his hand.

Just the first time that someone was Mack.

"Yeah." Simon said slowly. "I think I'm gonna order some wings. I'll just wait here until you get back, if that's okay."

He tapped a cigarette out of the pack and looked over at Mack as he lit it. "What? Oh. Was *wings* the wrong thing to order? I never thought—"

"It's nothing. I will return."

Another slight warming under the amulet. Simon grinned, crocodile wide and just as sincere. Mack nodded once, his foggy cloak swirling around him as he dissipated.

Simon's grin dropped. Still that looming sense of something big.

Of darkness, rising.

He rolled his shoulders and reached for his cigarettes again, tilting the pack. Instead of a cigarette, he spilled a chicory stem into his hand.

In a moment, he'd be rendered invisible. Just a parlor trick, when a guy thought about it. The disturbing thing at the moment, however, wasn't his ability to vanish.

It was Mack. When had he become so...transparent?

Rubbing his amulet and the memory of the itch Mack's influence had caused, he touched the twig to the embered end of his smoke, exhaling the spell with a lungful of smoke. Something big was happening somewhere. Time to find that event horizon.

Funny thing about event horizons.

Simon took a bolstering breath before pulling open the door. To the naked eye, they look normal. Shiny, well-lit places that drew you in. You think it's your own volition, never realizing it's the gravitational pull of the big fricken black hole behind it.

He walked out of the bar, closed his eyes, and let his feet take him there.

It was a simple technique that was less magic and more simple-minded. He never fooled himself into thinking his feet had any brains. He knew it was the black hole of darkness that drew him. He respected it and he acknowledged it and he hoped he'd be able to get his eyes back open in time to keep from falling in.

Across streets, through traffic, around trash cans and utility poles and dumpsters. He walked for about thirty minutes without even peeking. All he had to do was open his mind and let the dark power do the rest. It wanted him to find it. A paperclip, he was, being dragged to a magnet the size of the moon.

Easy as sin.

Then he stumbled over his feet, or what he thought

were his feet; the next breath he took was tinged with a current that felt like electricity wrapped in cotton. He blinked and found himself in the center of a giant parking lot.

And he saw the darkness he'd been tracking.

There was no doubting it.

A hell gate. Here. On earth. In plain sight of the entire mortal plane.

No. It couldn't be. Every law of metaphysics ensured that a hell gate opening was the last thing a mortal on earth ever had to worry about.

And there it stood, all the same.

Hell gate. The very name inspired a special brand of terror.

Hell: everything one feared it might be, plus a shit ton that cannot even begin to be imagined.

Gate: a portal. A passage. A way.

He shook his head. Screw Kent. Screw academics. Screw Crowley's fricken ghost because less than fifty yards away stood a hell gate. He knew it in his gut. It resonated through the moral fibers of his very being.

The impossible was possible. It was real. And it was here.

His eyes stung from the acridity, even standing relatively upwind. How many nights had he sat in Kent's dusty library, listening to the old boy read his notes? His theories on hell gates were complex and fully-explored— probably would have made for a great dissertation. Well, you can take the man out of Cambridge but blah diddy blah, right? That was the trouble with those academic types. They always came off sounding so—academic.

But none of those lessons could have prepared him for this sight. Nothing.

Theories of hell gates had him envisioning great stone

arches with the fiery colors of satanic fire glowing within. A sense of architecture, of actual structure in a defined time and place. But this—

This was a rip in the air. A massive tear, like a great claw had just dug in and yanked down. The sky was split, the ground was scored. It was a violation of nature.

And from between the jagged edges of what had once been perfect Earth shone through a blackness that Simon not only saw, but also felt in the marrow of his bones. It wasn't a color. It was a void. It had the shape of most grievous loss, it burned with the heat of a terrible lust, and it tasted like deepest despair.

That blackness looked out at him. It recognized him. And it smiled.

So much more frightening than flames or a devil waving a pitchfork. There, within the jagged edges of the hell gate stood a glimpse of true Hell—and Simon knew with frightened clarity that it was entirely personal.

Strange gases seeped from it, the elements of brimstone and hellfire. Those elements had no place on this plane. They blackened the earth surrounding the hell gate, poisoning the air, withering the grass.

What else would it kill? He didn't want to find out.

Sobered, he pulled up his big boy pants and cracked his knuckles. So. A hell gate was opened in Charm City. It was time to close that ugly bitch down.

He spread his hands, feeling for ley lines. Nothing more than a trickle, and even that came from a distance. At least the gate wasn't tapping into that kind of power source.

Dammit, Prof. Couldn't you have thought this through? All that talk about fricken gates and how impossible they were—

Well, the Prof had prepared him for this night, however inadvertently. Maybe it was time to go back to school and pull out his old lesson book. Hell gates weren't the only thing Prof had taught him.

He shrugged off his jacket, letting it slip to the ground. He unbuttoned his left sleeve and cuffed it in a series of quick flips, all the way up past his elbow. Had he known there was going to be a hell gate, he'd have worn short sleeves.

Oh, well. Magic wasn't always practical.

Maybe he could design a shirt with tear away sleeves, kind of like a stripper cop with a Velcro uniform, for those times when a mage wanted to dress sharp but didn't want his ability to wield magic hindered by cumbersome tailoring.

The tattoo tingled as if stimulated by the energy of the gate, a slight flush that warmed his skin. He rubbed the inside bend of his elbow, tapping it like a junkie. Turning his wrist, he tugged his wand free of its place beneath the strap of his wristwatch. Not like anyone wore a watch to tell the time these days.

He grimaced. This was going to hurt. Well, magic always had a price.

He stalked the perimeter of the anomaly, squatting at times, trying to get a sense of its dimensions. Needed to see the edges, see what direction it had been opened in. Hell coming out? Or someone going back in? He'd paced about sixty feet when he realized he wasn't moving around it. No matter where he went, it always looked the same. It was moving with him. Like it knew he was there and was squaring off at every step.

Not good. Simon scratched his head. If it had been a space-time thing, he could have warded it then pinched it shut by pulling the energy out of the sequestered area.

So much for that.

Maybe he needed a second opinion.

ROARRRRRRRR

A horrid sound grew around him, rumbling through him with a sinister vibration. The hell gate shifted. Activated. Simon groaned. He'd done it. He knew it. That tiny moment of doubt as half-intended as it was. Two-thirds sarcasm. Didn't matter. He had thought to himself that he needed help and the gate responded, sensing his weakness.

Quickly, he clamped down his emotion. Had to remain impassive. Emotions could get him killed.

Or worse.

Or...

He smiled, cold and cocky. It responded to weakness, did it? That might be a good thing. Because if it responded to one emotion, it would respond to another.

Simon pulled a tarnished silver compact out of his pocket. Flipping the latch, he dumped the herbal contents into his palm. The compact safely stowed once more, he cupped his hands together and rubbed, whispering a spell.

The herbs crumbled and atomized, forming a gritting cloud, hanging in the air just a moment. He centered himself before uttering the final word of the spell, which dispersed the herb cloud in a hum like a plucked cello.

His senses hitch-hiked on the enchanted herbs, his awareness expanding outward, down through the ground beneath his feet. Everything seemed intact, untainted, despite the proximity to a turnpike to Hell. Good. Anchoring himself to the earth, he envisioned the words of the chant he needed to wake the wand. The words appeared, one by one, in the front of his mind, lighting briefly like fireworks, burning themselves into his focused awareness.

He lifted the wand, gripped it like a syringe, his thumb over the hilt. Centering it above his tattoo, he readied the strike.

A sudden gale force wind smashed into him and blew the wand clean out of his hand. The hot ferocious gust twisted him into fighting to keep his balance. He nearly lost his footing. Almost went down.

The scalding rush of air carried upon it a scream. No, not a scream. A chorus of agonized voices, screams of pain that seared themselves into his soul, a sound unforgettable.

And above them all rose peals of laughter that curled the pit of his stomach.

ALLIANT.

His name, spoken by the one voice he had desperately hoped never to hear again. Bile soured his mouth.

The wand lost, his spell faded before he could use it.

I THOUGHT I SMELLED SOMETHING. YOU. I REMEMBER YOUR SMELL. THE SCENTS OF FEAR AND FAILURE. HAVE YOU COME TO BE DEFEATED ONCE MORE?

The laughter thundered through his head and he looked back to the gate and saw it, saw that fearsome countenance, and despair hit him like a truck.

Balazog stood within the maw of the gate, arms crossed and laughing.

Oh, he was a terrible sight to behold. The Corinthian, a general of Hell, enormous and scaled from head to foot. His armor was ancient but impenetrable. The leader of Hell's army needed no armor. Not when the power of Hell coursed through its rotten veins. Demons of that rank were legend.

Simon cursed himself for not cursing the demon.

ALLIANT. YOU CANNOT HELP YOURSELF. YOU HAVE ALWAYS RECOGNIZED TRUE POWER. YOU ADMIRE IT. YOU SEEK IT OUT.

YOU SEEK ME OUT AGAIN. WHAT PETTY TRIAL DO YOU HAVE FOR ME? WHAT PRETTY PRICE WILL YOU PAY?

Anger exploded like a pipe bomb deep in Simon's belly and it flushed him through. His cardinal rule forgotten. No emotion. Never anything the enemy could use.

His voice was ragged with hate. "You will leave this plane."

I HAVE NOT YET BEGUN TO MARCH UPON YOUR WRETCHED LITTLE PLANE.

Balazog chortled. YOU ARE WEAK. YOU ARE A PRETENDER. THAT IS WHY YOU CAN NEVER DEFEAT ME.

"I don't need to defeat you. All I need to do is shut you down."

YOU CANNOT.

"Like hell, I can't."

Simon thrust out his hand and forced the chant to reappear in his mind. It hurt, too soon after the last impotent summoning. Simon bit down, staring into the wretched eyes of the Corinthian, the mirrors of his eternal guilt, and decided it was time to give something back.

His wand, in his hand. Didn't know how, didn't matter. The spell surged into his mind, glowing like hot coils, re-igniting. He smiled, nothing cold about it.

Jabbing downward with the wand, he held his breath, bracing for the bite and the pain and the rush—

"Simon! Don't!"

His name called in a trill of fear. A child's voice. He choked, recognizing it immediately.

Balazog reached out through the gate. Simon stood, paralyzed by that voice, crippled. The demon wrapped his power around Simon and squeezed.

breath gone
pain exploded in his eyes
white around the edges
feet disappeared
knees hit the ground
face forward
mouth full of dirt

He flopped onto his back, rolled his eyes back to the gate. Blood tinged his vision bright pink.

Laughter. God-damned laughter.

Balazog leaned and smiled, the gleam of sharp teeth in a darkened face.

YOU ARE TOO USEFUL TO ME. WHICH PART DO I KEEP? THE PARTS THAT SCREAM? OR THE PARTS THAT BEG?

Simon drew up his knees and rolled onto his side, heaving a foamy cough. Gathering his knees beneath him, he pushed up, sitting on his heels, each breath a searing pain.

Fumbling in his pockets, he worked his Peruvian binding rings onto his thumbs. Looking back into the eyes of the abyss that would forever haunt him he chanted, a mumble that tasted like pennies.

"In the name of the Light..." He spat out a bloody mouthful. "I draw thee."

YOUR SPELL IS USELESS.

"In the name of the Light, I bind thee. In the name of the Light, I cast thee back into darkness."

I OWN YOU, LITTLE MAN.

"In the name of the Light, I command thee. Thou shalt do my will."

YES. BECAUSE YOU PAY ME WITH THE SOULS OF CHILDREN.

That was it. That was all he needed. That gave him the

strength to get to his feet and face his demon, even with all of Hell standing behind it. He didn't only have his magic and his training behind him.

He had Chiara, wherever she was. That made him a force to be reckoned with. "You know your place, you bastard. Your place is below."

NOT FOR MUCH LONGER.

"Go back to your place below!" Simon screamed with everything he had, his voice a ragged rasp, an old lion that would fight to the death surrounded by hyenas and staring down the monster that wanted its teeth in his throat.

He jammed the wand into his tattoo, his mind and his will and all he was or ever would be just laser-focused on one thing: get that hell gate shut and that demon's ass off his plane—

Something inside him ignited and just blew, like every fuse in the city exploding at once. His selfness swelled like a supernova. A tidal surge of power, his power, rose and took him on a headlong rush. He exceeded his limits too quickly for his mind to keep up. But when he did catch up to it...

Oh, the enormity.

Part of him laughed, child-like, open-mouthed, spinning on the razor's edge of infinity. He had no idea there was so much to himself. And it was him. All him. Of that, he was perfectly sure.

The other part, the part that didn't get swept up in the dizzying joy, smiled, harder and colder than he ever had smiled in his life. Harder, colder, solid absolution. He twisted his will like a flick of his wrist.

The hell gate, that wretched hole in the air, snapped shut, zipped closed with a boom that made his eyeballs thump.

The air cleared. The silence was deafening. The pressure in his chest exponentially increased and he choked, unable to breathe through the pain.

Simon was out before he even hit the ground.

Chiara stopped walking. Something was wrong with Simon.

She picked up her head and listened. No sound, no call that she could hear. But she didn't have to hear him. She could feel him.

This was different than the other night when she'd popped in to find him being accosted by that trashy demon. He'd sent out a curious vibe. She'd only meant to observe. Hadn't even planned on letting him know she was there. The possessed bar tramp was purely coincidental and she couldn't have remained hidden after it attacked.

No, this was different. He had just pulled off something massive. And, now, in the aftermath, he was fading.

She had to get to him.

Only one option. And it wasn't the easy way.

"Mack." She called out, her voice pitching higher with desperation. He had to hear her. "I need you."

The angel appeared, wearing a frown. At first she worried he would delay her with a lecture against summoning him.

Instead, he spoke first and she knew the frown wasn't

for her. "There is an unprecedented level of Hell-born interference. I cannot find Simon."

"I can," she said. "Use me and take us to him."

Without hesitation, he stepped up against her and wrapped his arms around her. In the arms of an angel. Nothing here to write sentimental songs about. This was like an iron coffin—

Then he opened his portal and her cynical thoughts whooshed right out of her mind as he yanked her through time and space. A purely angelic portal. Part of her resonated with it, hummed like struck silver, ringing with light and a wholesome chime.

Part of her rebelled, a hot fury that rebelled against the Light. It clawed at her insides, ripping her up. Anaphylaxis.

Her mortal body despaired, torn between the polarities of Light and Dark.

They landed, solid ground suddenly beneath her. She dropped to her knees, her stomach lurching upward into her throat with a nauseous surge. Swallowing a mouthful of salty saliva, she willed herself to keep composure. She would not give an angel the satisfaction of seeing her vomit. Sometimes, her mortal trappings were more bane than boon.

Wearily, she scanned the smoking ruins of what might have been a parking lot. Now, chunks of torn up asphalt littered the clearing, the scents of brimstone and destruction hanging thickly in the air.

A hell gate had been opened here.

But a mortal had closed it.

Only a split second later, she spotted them.

Simon lay sprawled, eyes closed. He looked as if a bomb had gone off in his pocket.

Broken. Smoke-stained and tattered. Disturbingly still.

Mack knelt by his side, speaking in low mournful tones.

"You let your anger take over, Simon. God could not help you because you turned your back on him when you gave in to anger."

Chiara hurried to them, kneeling down. The angel's eyes were bright with tears when he looked up at her. It touched her deeply, to see his concern.

"Why, Simon?" Mack stroked Simon's cheek and leaned to kiss his sooty forehead. "You literally handed yourself over to the dark and, in the dark, Balazog wins. Every time."

"Wait." Chiara's blood ran cold, an unfamiliar chill spilling down between her shoulders. "Bal did this?"

Mack looked up at her with sorrowful eyes. "I cannot help him here. Neither can you. But you *can* help him. Take him to your home. Do what you must. Please. Don't let him die."

Chiara nodded and she tried to swallow past the lump in her throat. "Take us as far as you can."

She slid her arm under Simon's limp neck and shielded him. Mack spread his arms, the ghost of his wings unfurling. Surrounded them both with his embrace, he opened the portal again.

She knew he did his best to be gentle. She was grateful, at least, for that.

Mack got them as far as her front door. Whether he used her as a guide again or had simply already known the location of her lair didn't make a difference now. All that mattered was Simon.

She carried him inside, past the couch he scorned, up the stairs and down the hall to the bedroom he favored. She washed his wounds, binding them in strips of a torn sheet. No first aid supplies were to be found in this house. Never had been, never would.

When she'd done all for him that she could, she waited.

She curled into a ball in an armchair at his bedside.

The sun rose and fell before he stirred. Little more than an eye blink in her long lifespan, yet it felt like the cruelest of eternities.

"Hey." His voice was quiet, and ragged, but steady. "Fancy meeting you here."

"Simon." She was at his side in an instant, gingerly sitting on the edge of the bed, careful not to jostle him. "Are you in pain?"

"Not the kind you can fix, sweetheart."

"You underestimate me." She brushed her fingertips over his hands, avoiding his raw knuckles. Scrapes and bruises everywhere, a thousand tiny hurts to add to the great, serious injuries.

"No. I don't." He leaked out a breath between pursed lips, his complexion pallid beneath his dark brows, black hair plastered to his forehead. "That's the problem, you see. I'm what you'd call beyond help."

"No." She put steel into her tone so that he'd believe her, even if she doubted herself. "You've come back this far. We'll get you the rest of the way here. Your supply trunk, the one in the van. Tell me how to retrieve it. You can…charm your way back."

"I think my luck has finally run out, kid." He sighed and looked at her, eyes unusually bright. "I finally crossed the line."

"You've crossed plenty of lines and yet—"

"This was a new one." His voice shrank, tiny and vulnerable. "I saw it."

Something in his voice made her sit up, wary. This wasn't like him. This sounded suspiciously like—

Like fear.

She reached for his hand. A brush against his wrist betrayed him if his voice hadn't already. His pulse, thread but quick, like a rabbit. Fear.

"Hell isn't a lake of fire." He squeezed his eyes shut, as if trying to unsee something. "It's a state of complete awareness, and perfect moral clarity, and an absolute absence of mercy. You know everything you ever did, and every person you hurt, and every mistake you made, and you get all that regret and sorrow all at once, and there is never release from it. The pain, the suffering, the desperation—that's you, for eternity. That's what Hell is. It's all yours."

He looked up at her, his eyes sunken, dull. Lifeless. Hopeless. "And I saw mine. I saw what's waiting for me."

It tore at her heart to see him so...broken. "You are not meant for Hell, Simon."

"I'm not going to Heaven, Chiara. My credit rating sucks." He stared at the ceiling, his expression slack, very much like a man in front of the gallows, waiting to be led up the stairs. "It takes a lot to get 'summoning demons to take revenge on high school bully' off a guy's rap sheet, not to mention what happened to Sarah."

"Simon..."

"Hey, kid. Cheer up. I promise I won't take you down with me. Now, I hate to be rude, but... I'm having trouble focusing on your face. I'm just gonna close my eyes for a while."

"Okay. But just a nap. Then you'd better wake up."

He closed his eyes, lashes dark against his wan cheeks. "Trust me. I'm too scared to die."

His breathing rose and fell in shallow but quiet puffs. If it had been her, she'd be healed already. She would have visited the pool and she'd be whole and on her feet and back to work.

Not Simon. He had two broken ribs and a bruised lung that would most likely keep him from smoking for a week or two, at least. The blood that had collected in the corners of his mouth made her suspect it had originally been collapsed. Perhaps the trip through the portal cauterized it.

He was lucky to be alive.

When they'd found him, he was sprawled within a circle of scorched earth that was littered with dead insects and more than one fallen bird. That hell gate should have killed him. Balazog almost did.

She closed the door, pausing outside to listen for a sign that the stubborn fool wasn't merely pretending to sleep, that he'd ignore her orders to stay in bed.

But there was silence. Simon must truly be exhausted if he didn't defy her just a little bit. She chewed her lip, knowing there was no more she could do except wait and watch over him.

For a brief moment she envied the mortals. At least they had someone to whom they could pray.

All she could do was hope. It was a different thing altogether.

She went downstairs and curled herself into a corner of her couch, tucking her blanket in around her feet. The fire blazed from the fireplace, as it always did. Its warmth failed to reach her.

He deserved better. He took beatings on a weekly basis in the name of the Light. He was their best hope to quell the rising dark. Anyone else would have considered it working toward redemption, or investing in a healthy plenary indulgence.

Instead, he'd resigned himself to all the slings and arrows the world and the divinities could throw at him, as if all of it were punishments he justly deserved.

What he deserved was to be sheltered, to be thanked. Instead he lay battered and broken and blaming himself for a hell gate he didn't open, a hell gate he never believed could possibly exist. He blamed himself for not being able to handle it better.

He'd saved Baltimore. He'd done what no other mortal had even attempted, let alone succeeded doing. He'd shut a portal that had been gated by the Corinthian himself. And all Simon was doing at the moment was taking his lashes.

Chiara stared at the fire, wanting nothing more than a nice little talk with her father. She wanted to rage against the Light for not making it clear to Simon just how valuable he was.

And part of her felt more than a trill of concern because upstairs lay a man who had more power than any mortal had ever shown before. Men did not manipulate gates. Period.

Simon had a power that no man should have. He truly was dangerous. Did he even know?

A sound outside in the hallway drew her attention. Something was outside her apartment. She slid off the couch, using her senses to scan the rest of the building. Nothing. No animal, no mortal. She knitted her brows and concentrated. No demons, either. After a hesitation, she pulled open the door to her apartment and peered out.

Mack stood in the far corner of the landing, his face lit in eerie lights from the hallway below.

She heaved a sigh and leaned against the doorway. "Trying to scare me?"

"Simply watching. It is what I do."

"You could do it without the suspicious noises."

"I did not know how to obtain your notice. Is he...?"

"He's sleeping." She crossed her arms. "But he needs more than sleep."

"A doctor."

"He needs peace, Malachi."

Mack bowed his head, recognizing his proper name.

She'd gleaned it when he took them through the portal. Poor spirits. Angels truly were subjects of the lowest form. Empty vessels, waiting for direction from someone else's Will.

"I see his unrest," he said. "I feel it trembling off him in waves. It is a terrible feeling, as great as any suffering I'd ever witnessed. But I cannot ease it. It is all connected. His weakness and his strength. And we need his strength."

"But—can you take the edge off it, just a little? Surely you can spare him some comfort without altering his fighting edge."

"No. I cannot."

"You mean, you will not." Her voice trembled, anger simmering. She was coming to a boil inside. She clenched her fists without thinking. "Selfish Light. Never worried about the mortals. You only drive them to satisfy the desire of the divine."

"You should not speak of things you don't understand."

"Oh, I do understand. I know what it's like to lose a parent and I know that it's a pain I could have lived without."

"He must leave the past behind him."

"Oh, have some compassion. You probably never stopped to think about what he must be feeling. What baggage he's carrying. He just lost his mother!"

"No." Mack looked at her oddly, a tilt of his head. "I do not think so."

"You don't think what?"

"He did not recently bear the loss of his mother."

"He wouldn't lie—"

"She has passed over. But her soul ascended nearly three years ago."

"But— Simon had said the authorities wanted him to tend to her estate. But if she died three years ago... Then why are the police searching for him?"

"He needs to answer that. I am neither a keeper nor a dispenser of his secrets." He stepped backwards into the fog that gathered behind him. "I am only here to watch."

She went back upstairs to check on Simon. When she opened the door, she was assaulted by a cloud of pungent smoke and the sight of Simon sitting on the edge of the bed, pulling on his jeans.

Her jaw dropped open. "What on earth are you doing?"

He stood to pull up his pants, a sharp intake of breath as he fastened them. "Not taking it lying down. Somewhere a hell gate is going to open again and I've got to be there to stop it."

"In your condition? An hour ago you were barely breathing."

"As you can see, I'm feeling much better." He turned with a flourish of outspread hands. "Thanks to a little help from an Inuit shaman, who taught me to never leave home without an emergency kit. I just needed a little aroma therapy."

He crumpled a little, hugging his rib and coughing softly, looking like a good cough would really hurt. He waved at the layer of heavy smoke that still hung in the room. "Open a window and it'll clear right out."

"You're not better. Get back in bed."

"I'd be better if I can have a dip in your ugly little pool. That stuff made you whole after you nearly bled out." He gingerly rubbed his ribs. "I just need a teaspoonful of it to finish things off."

"It's not kind of pool."

"Fine. I'll swim, then. I just don't like going under.

Water in the ears—*bleargh*."

"No, Simon." She shook her head with two tight jerks. "It's not a healing pool. It's…"

"It's…?" He prompted her with a roll of his hand.

Defeated, she sighed. "It's a portal. To my father."

"Finally!" He clapped his hands together, looking both furious and delighted. "A truth I can use. Maybe it's time I met your father so I can ask him about that hell gate I had to shut down."

She planted her hands on her hips, wanting to throttle him now that he was well-past the danger of dying. "Such self-preservation. You don't really care if you get yourself killed. What are you thinking, Simon?"

He just smiled, hard and dangerous. But his eyes held the truth. Pain. Self-loathing. He'd never run out of ways to punish himself because he'd never run out of reasons why he deserved it.

"You want to go? Fine." She grabbed his hand and got nose to nose and narrowed her eyes. "We're going."

He jerked his head away, suspicion in every line of his face. "Going where?"

"To Boston." Without releasing his hand, she strode from the room, pulling him behind. He was dead weight. Such a stubborn person.

Well, so was she. She leaned into the dragging, giving it a divine nudge. That made him move.

"No, no, no, no." He dragged his feet. "Thousand times, no."

Truly? She cast an impatient glare at him. He talked so big. Little big man thought he'd march up to her father, did he? Demand answers? Wave his fistful of charms at him? Oh, he was just a colossus of courage, wasn't he?

Until she mentioned Boston. Then the façade shattered. One thought of facing his past and he wanted to hide under the bed.

No. Not this time.

"Yes, we are." It took very little effort to pull him along behind her. He was in no shape to put up much of a struggle.

Panic made the edges of his voice brittle. "You have no idea what happened there."

Down the steps, out the door. Out of the street, she released her hold on him, knowing the three flights of stair would have robbed him of any desire to flee. She stepped to the curb and stood on her toes, scanning the traffic. "I know enough. You are stumbling in the dark, Simon. You're trying to forget who you were. You haven't forgotten her."

"Going to Boston with you isn't going to make me remember who I am. It'll just remind them. I don't want them to remember me."

She waved toward an oncoming taxi.

"Too late for that, I'm afraid." A cab slowed and she pulled open the door. "That hell gate was proof they haven't forgotten you."

On the flight, Simon drummed his fingers, grimacing at the scowls from the passenger beside him. Thirty thousand feet between him and the ground made him nothing but nervous. And what kind of magic kept these buses in the air? Nothing but bad juju.

At least they offered anesthesia. Several empty bottles stood on his tray table already, and the flight attendant was only halfway up the aisle. Ah, well. He'd catch her on the return trip.

Now, if there was only a way to charm her into letting him sneak a cig in the john...He sighed. Fricken underwear bombers. Had to ruin things for everyone.

Chiara patted his hand. "We'll be there in just a little bit."

He banged his head back against the head rest. "This is a nightmare."

"You worry too much."

"I don't worry enough, apparently. I'm charging headfirst into an ambush with a girl who wears a huge target."

"Shh. You're so pessimistic. Better watch yourself.

They'll try to use your shadows next."

"Let them." He gripped his armrest so fiercely his fingertips paled. "I'll be ready."

"No, you won't."

"Why are we doing this? For that matter, what exactly are we doing?"

She reached over and squeezed his hand, entwining their fingers. "You're a good man, Simon. And you're a good mage, dabbler or not. But your shadows make it too hard for you to see where you are going. When we get to Boston, we are going to banish that shadow, once and for all."

He closed his eyes. The way she made it sound, he just had a raging case of VD that could be cleared up with a course of penicillin. "It's not as simple as you make it sound."

"It never is. That's why you have to tell me about her. I need to know everything. You need to tell me."

Simon raised his hand that she held, their fingers still clasped. "Can't you just look in and see it? It would be easier than saying it."

"I did see what happened. But I need to hear your heart's side of the story."

Her eyes, so big and dark and forgiving. Would his secrets be safe with her? They'd never been safe with anyone. Not even the men he'd called *master*.

But she was more than they had been. She was more than a magician or a shaman or a priest. She was a special breed, a blend of impossible divinity. Breathing alchemy. The embodiment of everything that captured his imagination. The men he'd called masters would crouch at her feet and beg for enlightenment, for protection, for a brief glimpse of possibility.

And she had saved his life. And she held his hand. And

she asked him to trust her.

Simon took a deep breath and started telling the story he had never stopped reliving, every day, every fight, every night in his darkest nightmares.

"I was a stupid kid, who grew into a stupid teenager. I was no different than any other. Loud music. Smokes. Anything to seem cool enough. And there were stories, you know, about Salem and magic, and the bitchin' things you can do with it. Me and my friends, see, we got our hands on some old books. Journeyman's spells. Basic shit."

"How basic?" Her voice was even, non-committable. Non-judgmental.

So far. It was still early on.

He scratched the back of his neck. "Bend to my Will, Fire Starter, that sort of thing. They never thought anything of it, and neither did I, at first. Long after the others forgot about it, I still practiced. I had something inside that was trying to reach out, and magic was the only thing that allowed me to reach in." He held up his hands, fingertips not quite touching. "I needed to make that connection, complete that circuit. So I practiced. I used to do tricks for the kid that lived next door. Sarah was nine, maybe ten. Used to look out her window into mine at night and I'd make something float, or appear in her room. The way she'd laugh—It was a game to her."

"Magic is never a game," Chiara said.

"Yeah, well, tell that to a stupid kid trying to impress a girl. Casey was a year ahead of me in school. Cheerleader. Theatre club. She was the girl every guy would have killed for a single kiss. But she was mine. She wouldn't have given me a second look if I hadn't conjured. That caught her eye. Made her think I was special. Made me think I was special, too. Until she left, for another. He had money. Guess the poor kid with the magic tricks wasn't enough. And the sod that took my place, well. I'd already lost her. He won, him and his fancy car. He didn't have to do what he did."

The memory of the shame he'd endured, the abuse. Five against one was a coward's game, an ambush. He clenched his fists, his teeth so hard the cords in his jaw bulged. And the way she laughed at him the next day in school…

"Well. I wasn't going to let him get away with it. He could have her, the trashy bitch, but he wasn't going to take my self-respect. I showed him who had real power. I went home, I got my book. I went to the park where they hung out, the hoodlums. I opened a circle, I conjured—"

"Oh, no, please say you didn't."

"I did. I was angry. I was beyond angry. And stupid, stupid me hadn't yet learned that a circle drawn in anger can only do one thing."

Her voice was a strangled whisper. "A demon."

"Not just any demon."

Chiara lowered her eyes. "Bal. That's how you knew him."

"You got a real thing for the nicknames, doncha? Well, your buddy Bal, he did the trick, alright. He hunted down that bullying bastard and tore him to shreds right in front of me. And I enjoyed every minute of it. Dick bag deserved it."

"Did he?"

"Back then, he did. And you don't need to try to make me feel bad because I have been paying for it ever since. See, Balazog performed the task he had been summoned to perform, and when he was done, he wanted to be paid for it. And he took his pound of flesh, and all the smiles that went with it—"

"Sarah."

He rubbed his eyes, feeling old, feeling tired.

"He didn't even kill her first. He took her straight back to hell with him, body, soul, life, breath. An eternity of torment for a little girl who never did anything but laugh at my stupid tricks. I tried to fix it. I studied. I apprenticed. I exhausted master after master and I know more dead master mages than there are living ones now. I alienated my friends, my family. They thought I was crazy. Mom had a breakdown when she thought I was ready for the nuthouse. She thought she failed me. All I wanted was to know one thing, how to correct one mistake. But I never learned it. And now what am I but a stupid man, making the same stupid mistakes again and again?"

Chiara just nodded and rested her head on his shoulder.

"That felt too much like a confession," he said.

"Confession, I hear, is good for the soul."

"Then why don't I feel any better?"

She tilted her face up toward his. "Don't you?"

He didn't reply.

"You have carried a lot of guilt for a very long time. Was this the first time you expressed regret? Sorrow? Being angry with yourself, blame—those things aren't contrition. You know you would never make that mistake again. You know deep in your heart that you will never again be that cocky when an innocent life is at stake. You've done your penance. You can heal. And you've also told me everything I need to know to correct this."

"You can't correct this one, love. The demon that has her is too strong."

"He is. But I'm stronger."

"You're not even full demon."

"Thanks for noticing." She grinned at him. "Anyway, I

have a little something up my sleeve. You're not the only illusionist, you know. I'm holding all aces."

"You're starting to sound like me. And that's never a good thing. I hope you know what you're doing."

"Of course, I do." She pursed her lips and wrinkled her nose. "Mostly. I just have to sort the details."

Simon rubbed his mouth. "You have no limits."

"Oh, I have them. I just know where they are. See, people who don't know their limits spend their lives walking in the dark, all cautious, hands out, creeping one slow step at a time. They're too afraid they will come crashing hard against their limitations, like smacking into a wall. If they knew their limits, they'd be like kids in one of those inflatable bounce houses, jumping around like they could just about fly. And if they bounce into a wall, they see it coming, they turn a shoulder, and they realize it's not hard at all. Me, I know my limits. I know exactly how far I can go and I have the freedom of having my entire being available to use."

"Must be nice."

"It is. You'll see what I mean when we get you there."

"Not me." He rolled his head away. "I've gone much too far the way it is. All I want…is to go back."

"We are."

He smiled and squeezed her hand. She didn't know what he'd meant. Didn't matter. He loved her for getting pretty close.

No one had ever been brave enough to even try.

Simon rented a Honda at Logan International Airport and drove to a motel on the edge of Malden, about twenty minutes outside of Boston proper. Not like he planned it. He wasn't even really conscious about doing it. The roads just rolled their way beneath his wheels, the rotaries and the narrow streets that only a New Englander could love. (And, by *love*, he meant *navigate daily without resorting to vehicular homicide.*)

The motel was a two-storied stretch of rooms with a triangle-shaped parking lot that made no fricken sense at all. At least Chiara didn't comment on the chain-link fence that ran around the back of the property. Keeping someone out or something in? He had the same doubts.

They both just sort of squinted out the window at it a while before shrugging and getting out. Good a place as any. Wasn't like they would be here forever.

He read a handful of online reviews while they waited for the desk clerk to get off the phone. Non-smoking rooms, huh? He'd see about that.

Last room on the top floor. As private as it got. At least the foot traffic would be minimal. He ground out his smoke on the cement floor outside the door before he unlocked it, sweeping his hand with a gentleman's bow. "Your suite awaits, milady."

"Of course, it does," she said, her voice echoing from within. Odd. Commercial carpeting and ugly bedspreads in cheap motel rooms didn't usually lend itself to echoes. He peered around the doorway.

Her usual palace. Cruddy couch included.

Told you so was all she'd said. He smirked right back at her. See? Non-smoking room, his ass.

"Well, what's the plan?" He slouched on her sofa, blowing a smoke ring, wondering what the neighbors would be able to hear through the walls.

"I don't know. I guess I just want to see the area. I want to see all the good and beautiful things there are to see." She clasped her hands against her chest, spinning to face him. "You grew up here, didn't you? Give me a tour. Tomorrow is soon enough for everything to go to Hell."

"True enough." His gaze turned vague as he stared at the fire. "Although Hell usually isn't considerate enough to wait."

He intended to take her into Boston for a full-on Liberty Trail tour, men named Ebenezer wearing knicker pants and tricorn hats. Baked beans and Irish pubs and cannoli up in Little Italy. Maybe a harbor or two. The whole nine.

But not Salem. He was immovable on that particular point.

It should have been a straight shot down Broadway but he took the back way to town. Old habits. The back way turned out-of-the-way and the next he knew he was driving down the block upon which St. Berenice stood, the stone fortress of Twelve Steps and Plastic Cutlery. Simon slowed down and slouched in his seat as they passed, trying unsuccessfully not to look at the building.

"You should just pull into the lot," Chiara said. "I know you want to."

Grumbling, he did so, parking close enough to the front door that he heard it slam when someone came out. Sounded different from here on the outside. He glanced up at the windows, wondering if he'd see any of the prisoners. Knowing the building wasn't the prison that held them.

"You've stayed here, haven't you?" Her voice broke his reverie.

"More than once. The first time, it was involuntary. This place used to be a psychiatric hospital. I got to stay in the lock-down wing around back." He waggled his eyebrows. "Criminally insane, so they thought."

"That's awful."

"It was what it was. That mug shot you liked so much? Followed by a stint here at the nut house. Nobody knew demons existed, much less how to summon them. Of course, I was the crazy one. No one believed Hell was actually real. The arcane, the occult...movie shit, nothing more."

"Sanitariums are terrible places," she said. Her expression clouded over like a sudden gust of storm, brooding and ominous. "Those poor wretched people, barely covered in rags, left to starve, preyed upon for the sake of medical advancement. Lobotomies. Relief from their demons, they called it."

She cast a scalding glare at the front door, as if this place were to blame for old injustices. "All a lobotomy ever did was cut off the part of the brain that let me communicate with the demon inside, that human connection that enabled it to listen to me. Lobotomies. A life sentence of possession, that's what they are. Those poor souls were damned once they tapped the spikes into their brain. The demon was contained, but only temporarily. Once the host rotted, the demon would vape out to find another open soul. And the sanitariums were full of them."

"Well." Simon shrugged. He eyed her suspiciously. "This place actually wasn't all that bad. What the hell kind of place were you at?"

"Well, it was a while ago." Her gaze drifted as she tried to think back. "What year is it now?"

"Not going to ask, not going to ask, definitely no way I'm going to ask." He shook his head. She'd dropped enough hints that she'd lived anything but an average mortal lifetime. "I mean, they hardly do lobotomies anymore, and even then most of those are accidental. Anyway, I think the term *sanitarium* has gone largely out of fashion."

He tapped a cig out of his pack but didn't light it. "Nowadays if you have a demon causing you trouble, they send you to rehab. Unfortunately, I've seen the whole twelve steps list and none of them directly address exorcism. Bah. Useless. They do have spa days, though, cucumber masks and hot stone massage and organic buffets. And Xanax. The Xanax is always good."

"Do you think you'll ever have to come back here?"

Will I ever come back here? Depends on what "here" is. He looked hard at the portico, squinting. "Probably."

"Really?" She sounded disappointed. "Do you want to?"

"Maybe." He rubbed his tattoo, an itch too deep to scratch. There was one "here" he'd never be able to leave, not entirely. "Maybe once they get a program that can actually help."

But, deep down, he knew. No program, no infinite number of steps could ever solve his problem.

All the magic in the work couldn't solve that problem.

Not when magic was the problem.

"Yeah, well. Anyway." Enough was enough. Looking at the windows he used to look out of really didn't do much for his perspective. As long as there was magic, he'd be its slave. End of story. He stretched his arm behind her seat so he could back out. "Idle hands are the devil's playthings. And I don't share my toys. "

They passed the afternoon touring colonial historical sites. Lexington and Concord afforded some distraction without the headache of Boston traffic. As they headed back on the Concord turnpike, she chatted about colonial Boston and Paul Revere and something that sounded more like gossip than historical fact. She was showing her age again.

He gave her the royal treatment and treated her to a frappe on the way back. That was when she really blew his mind. Kid acted like she'd been around forever but she never drank coffee over ice cream? He didn't know if it was the caffeine or the sugar that did it. She seemed so excited, so human. So much like a girl.

And that was how he wanted to think of her: just a moment in the now.

Not as the conglomeration of divinities, the child of an Enochian who banished demons with hell fire and blessed the damned with holy chrism. Not as the thinnest sliver of a mortal who was spliced between the Light and the Dark. Not as the woman who travelled through hell gates.

A last glance at the girl who, for the moment, was simply just a girl. Then he turned off the pike, heading to Belmont. It was time.

He couldn't put it off any longer. This road—hell, all roads—led to only one place: his old neighborhood.

He drove stoically, refusing to really see what was outside the window. He paused at a stop sign, waiting, waiting, waiting. For what? What could change? Nothing ever changed. No matter how many times he went back nothing ever changed.

He hit the gas. Couldn't spend a lifetime at a stop sign.

Halfway down the street, he passed an outdated white house, plain plastered, old shingles. Didn't even have to look at it to know it was there. He gripped the steering wheel, his knuckles white.

Chiara tapped on the window. "Wow. That one is stuck in a time-warp, isn't it? Such a picture-perfect neighborhood, then there's that thing."

"Just like life, huh?" The words slid out on edge, sharper than he meant them to be. "Outside is perfection but there's always a flaw somewhere. Always some blight keeping it from being perfect."

He drove to the end of the block and shifted the car into park. A broad field in need of a good mowing. An empty playground. Swings that rocked with the occasional breeze. Abandoned, desolate, void of the sound of happy children.

Alright, well, it was a school day. But still. Even the dog park was empty.

"This is it. This is where...Sarah was taken." He couldn't make his voice obey. No matter how he tried to sound strong, he could never get her name out without feeling like he had a fist around his throat. "It looks the same. How can it look the same? It's been a lifetime—"

Chiara got out of the car and came around to his side, tapping on the window. "Come on. You didn't come all this way to sit in the car."

He took as deep a breath as he could. Tough thing when the sight of a merry-go-round was enough to make a grown man choke on a sob.

He bit his lips and got out of the car. She linked her arm in his as they walked into the park. He knew she wasn't being cute. She was keeping him from turning tail and running.

Concentrating on his feet, he counted the steps. Each one was a miracle.

"Where did it take Sarah?" Her voice was soft.

He pointed without looking up. "There. The merry-go-round. I used to push her round, you know. I can still hear her laughter."

He shrugged away from her and rubbed his head. Her laughter. It echoed through his head, innocent. Menacing. Accusing him. "God, it won't stop."

Chiara grabbed his arms. "Simon. Look at me."

"Make it stop." He whimpered, pouring everything he had into his eyes so she would see it, so she'd believe him, help him. "I just want her back."

"Simon..."

"Give her back!" Grief made his voice ragged and raw.

He screamed up at the sky, the universe, the whole bloody lot of Creation, just needing the right one to hear him. "Give her back to me, you bastard!"

She shook him, hard. "Focus on me, Simon. Focus! You have to draw a salt circle, right on the spot where the portal was. Do you remember?"

Did he remember?

The laughter in his head snapped off like a switch. His vision cleared. His voice became like a stone dropped into a well. "I'll never forget."

He reached into his pocket and pulled out a sandwich bag full of salt. Biting off the corner, he poured it out in a stream, concentrating, murmuring, drawing out a circle.

Chiara walked around it, leaning over to inspect it. She nodded her approval. "Good. Now, I need a spell. Do you know how to open Solomon's Staircase?"

Simon crumpled the empty bag and stuffed it into his pocket. "Oh, you've got to be fricken kidding me. Building a Solomon's Staircase on a salt circle? Do you have any idea…"

His mouth snapped shut while he mentally completed the magical calculations. "You do. You want me to do the one thing that can't be done."

"Why can't it be done?"

"It's a hell gate. You want a mortal man to open a hell gate."

Her gaze shifted. "Not entirely."

"A staircase into Hell."

"Yes..."

"Hell gate."

"No, not the same. Hell builds hell gates. They're trying to get out. To create chaos. Unbalance. That's not what this is. We are fixing a wrong."

"You're rationalizing."

"Can you do it or do I need to find someone else?"

He scratched the side of his head. It was pointless to argue with the kid when she was set on something.

There had to be limits, though, right? Just because a girl has an idea in her head doesn't make it a good idea. "You do realize that it's a two-way portal?"

She tucked a loose strand behind her ear. "That's the point."

"Why, though?"

"Because I'd like to be able to get out again." Her lips stretched with lukewarm humor.

His heart leapt like it was kick started and banged in his chest, cold adrenaline washing down his legs. "Oh, no, no, no. You are not going down there. That's a death wish."

Chiara rubbed her hands together and looked away. "I'm fairly sure it isn't."

"I can't just go marching down there and expect to skip on back out." Simon started to pace, careful not to step in the salt. "I may be, ah, detained."

She raised an eyebrow in question.

He shrugged. "I put a few of those folks down there."

"And that is precisely why you're not going with me."

Simon grasped her arms and pulled her up to his face. His voice was ragged and weary, lacking all of the iron in his eyes, his set jaw. "I can't let you go alone."

"But you must." She gently extricated herself from his grasp. "Look."

Chiara ran her hands over his chest, smoothing his rumpled shirt before tugging down his collar. Reaching into his shirt, she tugged out the chain. His amulet dangled from the end, winking in the sunlight. "I'll wear this, see? You can cast an *Extemporanivis* spell on this and monitor me."

His tongue felt thick and dry. His amulet. She wanted

to take his essence into Hell with her. "And turning that thing into a GoPro is going to make everything all better?"

"As good as I can make it."

His indignation crumpled. That soft voice. So unlike the voice she used when he'd first met. "Why? Just—why this?"

"Because I don't have anything else to offer you, Simon. And I want to make you better. You deserve to feel better."

His gaze never leaving hers, he pulled the chain over his head, feeling the weight of the amulet in his palm. He'd never taken this off, not once, since it had been blooded. It was a part of him. It was his protection, his armor. "You can't go running into Hell and back for the sake of a guy's feelings."

"You're not just any guy. I need you."

Well. He rubbed his lips with the side of his finger, weighing the words. He'd heard them before, countless times from the most random of people. Something about the look in her eyes, the timbre of her voice, the *feel* of her. It all added substance to the words that had fallen so easily yet shallowly from the mouths of others.

Wordlessly, he looped the chain over her head, tugging her hair over it, smoothing it back. If he couldn't go along, he'd send the best part of him with her. There was no one else he could imagine wearing it.

"I would protect you with my life, kid. I guess this little piece of me will have to do."

She positioned the pendant so it lay flat below the hollow of her throat. It glowed with fierce swirls, the magic turbulent within, protesting. He simply lay a finger upon it and pressed it against her skin. The glow settled, acclimating to their common touch.

"Now." She scrutinized him with an up and down look.

"It would have been easier if you'd worn a tie. I think my scarf will make a nice receiver."

Simon's shoulders crumpled like a sullen teenager and his eyes slid sideways. "It'll look stupid."

"Good thing no one is watching. Now, get chanting."

Chanting, he could do. Simon charmed the necklace with a wave of his fingers and a few words in Macedonian while Chiara tugged the scarf out of her hair. He scowled, but charmed the polka-dotted strip of silk when she held it up.

Chiara licked her lips. "Now, the staircase, if you don't mind."

What could he do? His hands were tied. As much as he hated—really hated—the idea of her descending, he knew he didn't want to stop her.

It had been years since he'd known the taste of hope. It was nearly a dead memory but when he looked at her, straight in the eyes, he saw a light there that could only be described as hope. Normal people didn't have that special light in their eyes.

She had to be different. She had to be the one to change this path he was on.

So what else to do but cast the Staircase? If anything went wrong, he swore he'd go right down after her. It was his fate to suffer. Not hers.

Even if things went her way, he'd still be the man who opened a hell gate and allowed his friend to walk right through it. It was a new kind of damned for him.

He prepared to cast the spell. But first...he needed a boost.

"Close your eyes," he said.

She didn't even ask why. She only did as he asked.

It only made him feel dirtier than this part usually did.

He slipped his wand out of his pocket and pulled up his

sleeve. Clenching his teeth, he mouthed the chant, his voice little more than breath, and pressed the wand into his tattoo.

The magic surged through him like a wave of pleasure, one that rolled his stomach and made his arm throb. The pleasure turned to cramping. His mouth watered and tasted like sea water.

Heroin was probably easier.

He cast the spell before the world went sideways on him.

Within the circle, the merry go round shuddered and shook and flattened and folded in on itself with metallic clanks. The ground beneath it sank, leaving a stone spiral staircase curling down. A cloud of dust rose, bringing the stench of sulfur.

She blinked hard when she heard the noise. "That was fast."

It was easy. Too easy. He yanked down his sleeve before she could see the sullen glow. "Well. I have dabbled, you know."

She grinned and stepped to the edge, looking in. "One more thing. A Water Wall. Can you do that? Say, the third step down? That will give you enough time to close it if things go south."

He stowed his wand, his fingers still tingling from the hit. "Did I tell you I don't like this?"

She didn't respond.

He closed his eyes and spoke a verse. The staircase filled with water, brimming at the third step.

He spread his hands, one last plea. "I don't have to say it, do I?"

"Don't worry." She shook her head. "I will."

She stepped onto the first step and slowly went down the staircase. Her clothing floated on the water. She kept walking. Her hair floated. She kept on until she was completely submerged and didn't stop. No bubbles, no sound.

He reached into his inside breast pocket. Instead of a charm or an amulet, he pulled out a rosary.

Making the Sign of the Cross, Simon began to pray.

Chiara rounded the final steps and completed her descent into Hell. When her feet hit the scorched terrain, a wave of muffled thunder rolled across the acrid plane.

Her hair whipped about by chaotic winds, she strode across the red raging landscape. It looked like a battlefield, piles of bodies, mangled and maimed...

But not dead. Tormented souls, strewn all around, eternally trapped by their choices. Some reached out to her, pleading for help.

She didn't even look at them. She walked with a purpose, knowing exactly where she had to go.

Simon stood at the edge of the pit, her scarf tied around his forehead, eyes unfocused, watching Chiara from the view of the charmed necklace. He can see whatever her amulet pointed at, but cannot hear. He doesn't regret that caveat one little bit. Hell was a terrible noise to endure.

He saw the fields of Hell. He saw exactly what awaited him. He clutched the rosary so hard his hand bled on the Crucifix.

On a hill stood a monstrous figure, standing like a monument to the decay and the agony around it. As she approached it, the demon's shifting features come into focus.

And Simon knew exactly who it was.

Chiara marched up the hill, lesser demons snarling and slinking out of her way.

Balazog stood like a giant and marked her approach, chortling as she grew near.

WHERE IS YOUR PRETTY MORTAL FACE, NOW? YOU STINK OF THE ABOVE. YOU STAYED TOO LONG. YOU ARE SOFT AND WEAK.

"I am here for the girl."

Balazog bared his teeth, a lipless parody of a smile. *SHE IS MINE. MY VICTORY. MY WAGER. MY WIN.*

"She was not a prize. She was a smash and grab and she doesn't belong here. Release her to me."

Balazog crossed his scaled arms over his grotesque chest. *AND WHAT DO YOU OFFER IN TRADE?*

"I remind you of your allegiance."

MY ALLEGIANCE IS NO CONCERN OF YOURS.

"Is it not?" She paced a circle around him. "My word can find an eager ear. A misdirection, a tiny betrayal."

LIES ARE NOT THREATS HERE.

"No, they are tools. Soldiers are tools. You are a soldier. So are they all." She swept her hand around, indicating the ruins of hell, the shadows skulking across its scarred plains. "And those soldiers do not fight for you."

Balazog spread his tattered wings, the leather vulcanized by eons of purloined power and Hell's arid heat. Every battle, every vanquished foe, every tiny victory—all of it went into his armor, his wings, his hide. He was nigh indestructible. A true general of hell.

Chiara had no way to physically defeat him. Not on this plane, nor upon any other. And she was the offspring of two divinities. Balazog couldn't even claim that—demons were once mortal men before their damnation.

Oh, no. This wouldn't be hand-to-hand combat, even if Balazog planned on exactly that. She exhaled, opening her mind and beckoning to her father. His power filled her like a scalding wind.

The Corinthian reared back and slashed at her, seeking the tender flesh he'd rent before. She stood her ground and stared him down.

And when his claws glanced harmlessly off her, she smiled.

He roared and struck again. Claws slid right over her, throwing tiny silver sparks. His rage made him lose control and he lunged, grabbing her and throwing her down, throwing all his weight and his rage into it, pinning her beneath his talon-tipped wings.

Calmly, she gazed up at him, as beguiling as a lover. "You know your place. Your place is below."

I AM BELOW! he screamed.

She allowed her father's nature to roll to the surface. It was part of her, half of who she was. Even here in the heat of hell, buried beneath a hulking mass of general-rank demon, she felt clammy and cold. She nodded. "And you will never forget your place. I promise it."

Balazog sprang off her in surprise. She slid to her feet, fluid-like, serpentine-like.

The one-track mind of a warrior made him forget his surprise and he scrambled after her, clawing and clutching and gnashing his teeth upon her.

And she was unscathed. He should have filleted her, devoured her. And nothing. Nothing! His impotent attempts to hurt her infuriated him.

That was when she saw the first chink in his armor. The breastplate loosened and hung on its hinge. She rolled around him and whispered in his ear.

"You know your place." She stroked his face, the gnarled misshapen lumps of leathery face.

He screamed and grabbed her around the waist.

She twisted and slid free as if she'd been greased. Another show of silver sparks, another crack in the armor as the plate broke free and clattered to the ground. Each tiny defeat weakened him. More plates rattled and loosened.

"Your place is below. Stay in your place below."

Time and again he rushed her, desperation wearing through the rage. Each time she whispered his dreaded truth. Each time she evaded him, each time his hard-won armor weakened and crumbled.

Finally, he turned to her, his armor destroyed, his wings drooping, and he revealed what made him Simon's worst nightmare.

A small girl huddled, trapped inside his misshapen abdomen. Dirty and wide-eyed, the child looked driven to madness, holding onto the demon's ribs like prison bars. Her eyes peered out, searching wildly about.

When she saw Chiara, she screamed.

Simon couldn't keep up with the images that flitted through his Sight, streaming from the *Extemporanivis* spell. He saw the demon rush Chiara, saw her roll with the demon when he jumped her. But the action slowed and he caught his breath but then demon turned and he saw her, saw the child, trapped and screaming—

"Release her to me." Chiara closed her mind, feeling her father's influence fade. The heat returned like burning canvas, stealing her breath.

AND IN EXCHANGE?

"You survive. I bested you. The Corinthian is powerless against me."

A TRICK. I WILL KEEP YOU IN HER PLACE.

"Will you?" She smiled coldly. "I've no use for an empty threat. You cannot touch me. But I will acknowledge your power, general. I will not keep all the spoils. One pass. No more. One pass. By a minion—" She raised a finger, emphasizing the condition. "And no more than one soul. A deserving soul."

He shifted his stance. No one liked to admit defeat, not even in hell, where all were defeated from the moment they arrived.

WHY DO I THINK YOU WIN BOTH WAYS?

"Because my father makes the rules. Do we have a deal?"

DO I HAVE A CHOICE?

Chiara just smiled. "This is Hell, dearie. Choices do not exist here."

Balazog shuddered and clenched his fists. The ground trembled with the force of power. He shifted, distorted, his very body splaying outward and dispelling the child.

The girl stumbled to her knees, falling into the acrid dust, choking. Tears streaked her face. Chiara took the child by the hand and led her back to the portal.

Carefully, she knelt down in front of the girl. Sarah whimpered and twisted her head away, eyes squinched shut. "Don't hurt me. Please. I just want to go home."

Chiara gently squeezed her shoulders. "Sarah, you *are* going home. Right up those stairs."

"I can leave? I can finally…leave?"

The tiny hope that flickered in Sarah's, like a new firefly, was a good sign. Hell hadn't destroyed her spirit completely.

Chiara smiled and smoothed the girl's snarled hair. "You'll find someone waiting up there for you. He's pretty old now but don't be afraid. You'll know him."

Sarah hiccupped and nodded. Chiara hugged her and turned her toward the stairs. She lifted Simon's amulet over her head and placed it around Sarah's neck, repositioning it on her chest before urging her forward.

The child took each step hesitantly, not quite trusting. Her tenure in Hell had killed her hope, replacing it with despair...and suspicion. Sarah ascended slowly, eyes on the brightness above. She never looked back.

Chiara didn't follow the child. Instead, she turned back to the landscape of smoke and pain. In the distance lay an iron road. She set off toward it.

Simon's vision refocused when he saw movement on the staircase. Pressure in his chest squeezed his breath to a standstill when he saw who it was.

Sarah. She broke the surface of the water and emerged dry, eyes flitting everywhere, shoulders hunched.

"Sarah." He slipped his lens out and held it to his eye, hand trembling. Through the glass, she appeared normal. Perfectly normal. "No. Can't be. Sarah?"

"Simon? Is that you? Simon!" Her eyes grew wide and she smiled, ear to ear. She raced to his arms and clutched him, squeezing his waist hard enough to hurt his still-bruised ribs.

Solid arms, not the phantom of another dream. She was real. Still ten years old, still a smile that could knock a guy off his feet. Still Sarah, here.

The past had been undone. Almost every regret he'd bourn in his heart, forgiven.

He pulled her back and knelt, looking hard at her,

cupping her sooty chin. She was real. Chiara had saved the child. Saved them both. Not a ruse. Real—

Then he saw his amulet on her chest.

Chiara.

She was still down there.

He held the child to his chest and stared over her shoulder to the empty staircase, horror stopping his breath.

Chiara followed the iron road to a great fortress. Stone walls spanned out to infinity, too high to climb, too wide to circumvent. The road had led her inevitably to a massive and heavily guarded door.

Legions of faceless demons stood in rank before the door. An army that could strike the stoutest heart dead with fear.

At her approach, they turned and stepped aside as easily as stirring flower petals on the surface of a puddle. Admitted her without a fight. Why would they fight her?

She raised a finger and pushed the door open, the effort using more will than force. The inside was lit by torches in iron sconces. Even inside the windowless fortress, there was more light than had been on the dim Hell plane. Eternal twilight, fear of the dark. Here, hellfire provided the comfort of light.

Ironic. Then again, Hell had a thing for ironies.

Once inside, there was only one way to go. She exhaled through her nose and eyed the staircase.

Down.

Deep into a winding dungeon, she trudged for an immeasurable length of time. Minutes and hours and days didn't exist here. In Hell, there was only one measurement of time: forever. It always felt like forever.

Eventually the stone stairs and stretching corridors ended, and she faced a massive iron door.

She raised her finger again and drew a symbol across the corroded metal. Internal mechanisms whirred and clanked and the door clacked open, swinging wide with a creaking groan.

Music seeped out, sounds of a string quartet. She stepped into the same room as her own palace, with identical décor.

Nearly identical. One difference. Instead of a couch, there was a throne.

A tall man in an elegant suit stood near the fireplace, His back to the door, holding a glass of wine. He turned His head as she walked toward Him.

His eyes lit up, hot white coals, and He smiled. A selfish, wicked smile.

"So. The Halfling returns and marches into hell, undaunted. Come, let me have a look at all your ruined perfection." He turned, opening His arms. "Welcome home, daughter."

She scowled at Him. "There is nothing ruined about me."

"Sweetheart, you were born ruined. Marred by humanity and angel stink."

"I was born perfect. I have always been perfect. I do what I must do, perfectly."

Lucifer set down His glass on the mantle and walked over to her, wrapping His arms around her, kissing her tenderly on the cheek. "I could make you perfect. I could burn away those imperfections, like purifying precious metal. All you have to do is accept your place here."

She didn't return the embrace. Instead she shrugged

away. "I'm not staying long."

"You say that every time."

"I mean it every time." She drifted away from Him, rubbing her hands.

Lucifer tugged His cuffs, adjusting His suit jacket. "You know I don't approve of your consorting with that criminal, Alliant. And I like criminals."

"He is not a criminal, Father."

"He is wrong for you."

"He is not for me. No one is." She turned her head only enough to look at him, a baleful heaviness dulling her eyes. "You made sure of that."

Lucifer clucked His tongue and took up His glass again. "Come, now. We all have a destiny."

"Oh, don't lecture me on destinies. This was not yours."

Without warning, Lucifer slammed His glass on the floor, shattering it. The entire room shook and distant thunder rolled. "Don't you dare! This is my kingdom and you, my dear, are royalty, no matter how unwilling you act. Tell me you don't enjoy the perks of being daddy's little girl."

"I don't like owing you."

"You are my child. You don't owe me." He straightened His tie and tugged His jacket straight. "I provide."

"It's never that simple with you."

"Because you don't trust me."

She wanted to grumble at Him. The entire journey here, she anticipated facing off against Lucifer, king of Hell. Living in the mortal world, it was so easy to think of Him as the stereotypical Fallen One, the enemy of God, the archon of eternal darkness.

But it never went that way. There was never that ultimate moment of confrontation. She always ended up face to face with her father. And that always made it

harder to maintain her resolve. "You don't exactly have a
sterling reputation."

"That's business. You're personal. I don't need to treat
all the world the way I treat you. When are you going to
realize that?"

"When you can prove to me that you can play fair."

"I do play fair, dearest. The trouble is, you are
confusing the rules of one game with another."

Chiara looked away.

Lucifer softened His stance. "Look. I'm glad you're
here, even if it's only for a moment. But we do have to talk
about that little deal you made out there."

Simon pushed the girl behind him and turned back to
the edge of the portal, shouting Chiara's name. A
movement stirred below.

He leaned over the portal, hands on his knees. "Chiara,
honey, come on, come on, come on…"

The movement below rose up the stairs like a bur.
Chiara, running at top speed, looking like the hells were on
her heels.

When she hit the water barrier, she stopped. Eyes wild,
she sought Simon's face. She banged on the ceiling
trapping her, using both her fists. Her mouth moved
silently, sound cut off by the magical barrier. *Let me out! Let
me out!*

Simon stood up to his full height and stared her down.

Sarah crept behind him, holding his waist, peering out
from his side. "Who is that, Simon?"

His brows furrowed. "I… don't know."

Chiara toyed with a small sculpture on a pedestal. In her
version of home, it would have been a replica of the
Frudakis Freedom sculpture.

176

In Lucifer's version, it was different. The sculpture looked like a wall built with the bodies of dying men, a great horned beast standing triumphant over them. She curled her lip in distaste. "What's to talk about?"

"Simply an opportunity to express my admiration. I saw what you did with my Corinthian. You let him think he won something that would have been his anyway. He's shrewd and he's greedy and yet, you bent him to your will. Well done."

"Are you angry with me?" She averted her gaze. A punishment was looming, she could almost feel it. By opening herself to his influence, she'd borrowed a part of him without permission. She knew he didn't like being pilfered.

"No," He said. "Not mad. Concerned."

She turned toward him, not trusting her ears. Words meant little here. True value was measured in intent and conviction.

"I haven't given you an easy destiny." He walked over to His throne and sat, His elbows on His knees. "You've always done well walking the line between the Light and the Dark. It was my hope for you when I Named you. But if you start doing things my way, your mother will find out. And that would be...most undesirable."

She swallowed, her throat suddenly sticky. "Where is she?"

"That's the problem. I do not know." He raised His head, slowly shaking it, His upturned brows giving Him away. "Watch your back, daughter. I can't always be there to protect you."

Simon planted his feet and braced himself against the trembling of the ground. The water surface rippled with each smash from Chiara's fists.

He stood stock-still, his eyes glassy and unblinking, and made no move to dispel it.

Not even when she clutched at her throat, appearing to choke. Bubbles escaped her mouth as she continued to cry out for release.

And all he did was pull out his cigarettes and lip one out of the pack.

Her face shimmered, shifted, changed. The bones slid under her skin, which withered and blackened until she was nothing more than a demonic minion.

Rat-faced, ragged, and red-eyed, it shattered the barrier and shot out of the portal with a horrific scream. Simon hunched over Sarah, gripping her tightly, shielding her. The minion took off, leaving a streak of soot and flames that scorched the air in its wake.

Simon instinctively chanted the spell that would reverse the portal. The ground shifted and swallowed up the staircase as if it never existed, sealing shut with a slam that rocked him to his knees.

Chiara scowled like a teenager. "Mother is the least of my worries."

"She shouldn't be." Lucifer adjusted His collar. Funny how talking about Mother always made Him uncomfortable. "You forget, I know her very well."

She rubbed her arms, the discomfort mutual. "Well, right now, there are bigger problems."

"Such as…?"

"The Corinthian."

He laughed. "You bested him."

"*You* bested him. Through me." She drew a shuddering breath. "I want him bound."

"I don't understand."

"He gated, Father. To the Above. He tried taking a soul

and I stopped him, but just barely. Was that sanctioned?"

He didn't answer. His hooded gaze held secrets the way no mortal ever could. King of Deceit. Nothing more than a military tactic. "I noticed his brooding as of late. He will be difficult, I suspect."

"He must be bound."

"Why?"

Hands on her hips, she frowned at Him. The haughty royal, stamping her foot. "Because no servant should have that kind of freedom. He nearly killed me."

Lucifer scoffed. "You would not have died."

Her gaze slid sideways and she tapped her lip with a finger. "I did make it to the pool in time…"

"See?"

"…because Simon carried me there."

All the humor ran from Lucifer's expression, pulling His features down into heavy, stony lines. "The magician."

"Yes."

"The magician saw the silver pool." He placed a threatening emphasis on each word.

It was Chiara's turn for amusement. "Mmm-hmm."

"No mortal should know of its existence."

"I would have died if he hadn't. Would you rather I had died?"

He narrowed His eyes.

She climbed the three steps of the dais and grasped his hands. "Then Balazog needs to know that damaging me and subsequently revealing one of your many secrets is a punishable offence. Bind him to Hell. Remove his access to the mortal plane."

"He is powerful and well-known. Should a magician summon him—"

"Then the magician should fail. Irrevocable sentence, Father. Take his Name. Bind him, permanently and unequivocally. For the damage he has done to you."

Lucifer's eyes flashed silver, His anger breaking through. The vase on the mantle began to rattle.

That's right. Remind him again. Daddy's little girl, indeed. She could wind Him around her little finger. Sometimes, it was so easy to play His game. "And the damage he has done to me."

"What damage?" Lucifer scoffed. "You are stronger than ever before."

Yes. She was.

One thing she did not need to be reminded of. She'd lost another piece of her mortality when she healed in the pool. It had made channeling her father's essence so easy...

"Exactly." There was iron in her voice to stifle the rage, the despair, the slipping of her precarious balance. "And he's got to pay for that."

Lucifer rubbed His mouth.

"What are you planning to do? About him, I mean?" He lifted His chin as if referring to someone upstairs.

He was, in a way. "Simon? Nothing."

"Well, not right now. You've given him what he needs. He is healing." He glared at the ceiling as if He could see Simon. "He will be nearly whole. And I don't like him. I didn't like him when he was a fresh-faced apprentice. He was barely tolerable when he was drooling his days away in the nut house. And I will not like him whole."

"He is a human and out of your jurisdiction."

"Not entirely." Lucifer's eyes flashed again. "My darkness will rise."

"And the Light will be just as heavy. There must always be a balance."

"What there must be is war!"

"And you've already been to the general's tent. You

have already sat down and dictated the terms of that war. It's war by proxy, Father. I know the terms as well as you. War by proxy, fought amongst your mortal toy soldiers, no divine assistance or interference or persuasion. You agreed to arbitration. You are bound by the terms."

"Unfair terms. He encouraged his temples to be built. What kind of piece do I get to speak?"

"None, because it is not yet your time."

"I can bring about that time," He said, His voice little more than a growl. "I've waited aeons. All I have to do is show them who is the mightier, who is the wronged."

"There cannot be interference! You and all yours, and Him, and all His—keep your damned noses out of this. It isn't your war to fight anymore. It's theirs."

"You think it's not my business? This is personal, child. This is the very definition of personal."

"It's beyond you, now. What happened to you…it's too far gone to be of consequence anymore. It's not you versus Him. It's Light versus Darkness. That's all. It's so simple. Just let it go. Stop interfering."

"And what are you? You fight for the Light, while you reap all the benefits of the Darkness. What are you if not interference?"

"Then you shouldn't have given me humanity. That was your biggest mistake. You engineered me but you didn't foresee this. My humanity keeps me beyond your—and His—jurisdiction."

"You will obey me, Chiaroscuro." Lucifer sat back, straight and firm in his throne. The ruler, with eyes of silver ice and the shadow of leathered wings arching behind Him. "I am your father. I am the king of all darkness. I am Hell!"

She smiled thinly, trying to warm her eyes in the light of his cold fire. "But I am not. I am human. And I have free will. This isn't your war anymore, Father. It's mine."

She took both His hands and tugged Him to His feet. He bowed His head to her. She stood on her tiptoes, reaching up to kiss His cheek.

"And I'm going now. Goodbye, Father. I'll see you soon enough." She patted his arm gently before turning toward the door.

Lucifer watched her leave, His Morningstar eyes like quicksilver again. "Oh, yes, you will. You most certainly will."

Hand in hand, Simon and Sarah stared at the scorched earth where the Staircase had been. A lazy wind scattered the salt, destroying the circle.

His brain did a flat-line buzz for a moment as he struggled to comprehend—no, accept—what had just happened. He was the one who'd opened that portal, not Chiara. She couldn't re-open it.

It was his spell and he'd just shut it down on her, stranding her in Hell. Was this how God felt when He shuffled cards and dealt out judgments? Did God feel this dirty, this low, this despicable all the time? Was this to be his eternity?

"No, no. You can't be gone." He shook his head, wobbling on the edge of a soul-deep abyss, feeling the stones crumble beneath his feet. His shoulders crumpled and he felt the plunge coming. He knew it and he knew he deserved it. "You can't be."

A familiar sound, a clearing of throat, came from behind him.

He whipped around to see Chiara. A thin glowing line hovered in the air behind her. The remnant of a hell gate, fading like a gentle memory. But not her. She remained, firmly in their world.

His heart thumped, blood resuming its natural flow, warming his adrenaline-chilled limbs in a wash of heat. She survived. *He* survived.

"How did you—" Simon grabbed her up in a tight embrace, spinning her off her feet. "It's you. I know it's you."

She nodded, serenity settling upon her features as if she were allowing herself to relax, from the insides out.

What had she seen? Endured? Because of him? He felt shamed, dropping his gaze to the scattering of salt and expended magic, still smoking in the dirt at their feet. "I had to seal it. A lesser demon broke out. Smelled like minion rank, you know, that weird rotting onion smell they have but—I couldn't risk—oh, God."

He swallowed around a knot that wanted to choke him and courageously met her eyes. "Can you forgive me?"

"There is nothing to forgive." She laughed gently, as if she hadn't spent another forever in Hell, and cupped his cheek. "You did the right thing. Didn't he, sweetie?"

"That was you?" Sarah peered up at her, scrutinizing her from head to toe. "I like you better like this. You're prettier."

Simon rubbed his eyes. "I don't think I want to know," he said.

Chiara smiled at Sarah, ignoring Simon.

"I think so, too. I'm not one for extremes. Anyway." She cleared her throat and squatted down to Sarah's level. "How would you like to go home, Sarah?"

Simon just looked at her over Sarah's head, something heavy and unspoken in his eyes.

Chiara blinked rapidly, her eyes unusually bright and whispered. "Me, too."

Back at the hotel, next door to Chiara's suite—in a regular room—Simon went through the rituals of a series of complex catching-up spells.

Chiara paced outside in the breezeway, pausing to peer in through a crack in the drapes.

Mack sat cross-legged in front of the door, eyes closed. She knew better than to think he was asleep. She was pretty sure he didn't need eyes to see what went on around him.

A few hours into the vigil, he spoke. The sudden sound of his voice made her jump.

"That was a selfless thing to do," Mack said.

She crossed her arms and leaned back against the railing. "It was the only thing I could do."

"It had such a profound effect on him. Just look at him."

The sliver of light between the drapes didn't offer much of a view. Occasionally he would cross in front, hands raised, the muffled sound of his voice coming through the glass.

Sometimes, she didn't need eyes, either. She saw him with her senses, saw his aura. For the first time since she met him, there wasn't a jagged edge ripping through him, keeping his pieces from coming together, from being whole. He was healing, just as Father had said.

But unlike Father, she *did* like Simon whole.

Well, more whole. There was a weakness he kept hidden, even from her. It was a weakness he seemed unwilling to relinquish.

Time. He needed for time. And for a while, at least, they had it.

"What is he doing?" Chiara hooked a thumb over her shoulder toward the room.

Mack leaned his head back and opened his eyes. "He's assimilating her. She's been in Hell for seventeen years. She can't just scamper off into the world."

She crossed her arms, hugging her ribs. "When I looked in before, I didn't even recognize her."

"Well, he's helping nature catch up. The spell will rapidly age her body seventeen years. She's growing up right before our eyes. Then again, most mortals do that, don't they?"

She smiled gently, appreciating the sentiment. There were very few beings that shared Chiara's perspective, especially when it came to lifespans. "How is she going to live? A ten-year-old who suffered in hell for an eternity, thrust into an adult body—"

"There is a second spell. A much more difficult one. That's the reason I'm here—to guard him, to help him conserve energy and concentration. He's rebuilding her psyche. Seventeen years of manufactured memories and experience to write over her memories of Hell. He's giving her a real past."

"But time in Hell doesn't pass in real-time." A shudder ran through her, a chill that dripped down her back. She knew what happened in Hell and she didn't like dwelling upon it. "Her soul's been aged to an impossible point. Her soul can't be rebooted. Her innocence has been destroyed."

"Oh, ye of little faith," Mack said, his voice soft.

The minutes dragged past them in silence. The door clicked open. Simon wandered out and pulled out a cigarette, leaning heavily against the frame of the door. "What, a party and you didn't invite me?"

"How is she?" Chiara asked.

He shrugged. "Sleeping."

She peered through the open door and saw a figure

lying on the bed, eyes closed, a rosy glow hovering over her body like tinted valley fog. But the ten-year-old was nowhere to be seen. There was a woman, late twenties, lines etched near her eyes even in the relaxation of deep sleep.

He cupped his hand around his lighter, even though there was no breeze to disturb the flame. "She needs time to stitch her parts back together."

"Will she be okay?" she asked.

"As good as she'll ever be. You said it yourself, you can't unsee a divinity. She'll never lose the scars of inevitability or the certain knowledge of what lies beyond the mortal realm." He scrubbed his eyes with the heels of his palms before rubbing his head, leaving his hair in tousled spikes. "Eventually, the guises will break down and she'll remember. It'll start as a vague itch she can't put a finger on, that will grow into a conviction she can't prove. One thing is for sure. She'll be recruited by some paranormal team or another. But that's a bridge we can cross when we get there."

"So what's next?"

"What else? We get a good night's sleep and tomorrow we take her home. And..." He took a deep breath and gave her the full touch of his gaze. "We talk."

"About?"

"You opened a hell gate to get back."

Oh. There was that. She knew it would come up, eventually. Such a critical time as this needed complete honesty. "Yes."

"What price did you pay for it, kid?"

She blinked, taken aback. Of all the things she thought he'd follow up with, personal concern was near the bottom of the list. No accusation, no reprimand or disdain tinted his tone. And his body language was completely open.

He was worried about her.

She reached over and stroked his arm. "None of consequence. I promise."

"I don't know if you're lying to protect me or if it's actually the truth. In which case...I hope it's the lie." He grinned, lopsided and charming.

She returned the grin. Intuitive man.

Not long afterwards, Chiara stood watch over Simon and Sarah as they slept. He'd tried to eat something but said he was too tired to chew. He sprawled face down on the other bed and was twitching himself to sleep in less than a minute.

Chiara never left the foot of his bed, never let her guard down. Mack remained outside against the door. It was as safe as safe could ever get for a child who'd been rescued from Hell and the man who never gave up on the hope of getting her back.

It was an idyllic morning in Belmont. Birdsong and early morning traffic, dog-walkers and school buses. This was what life was like when Simon was sixteen years old, back when magic was more evident in the force of an early spring than in a kid messing with powers he didn't understand.

He pulled the car over diagonally from Sarah's parents' home and switched off the ignition.

Sarah hadn't said much on the drive over. What would she have to talk about? He'd only given her a muddled version of the last few days, just enough so that she could see straight and acclimate herself into the real world again. Not enough for police to interrogate before setting off on a misinformed manhunt for abductors who didn't exist. On this plane, anyway.

Chiara had bought her a new outfit that, thanks to current trends, looked sufficiently broken in. Her hair was in a hasty ponytail that looked like a little kid did it.

Well, technically…but that was neither here nor there.

There was a fat wad of bills in her jacket pocket, all the money he'd squirreled away over the years. Lean living, in more ways than one. It seemed a fortune to him now, only counted and realized the day Sarah came home.

Not that he needed to put a value on such things.

"Simon." She leaned around the Chiara's seat, waiting, watching the house. "I remember that house."

"See? Told you it would all come back to you. Can you picture the inside?"

She squinched her lips to one side and tilted her head. "A pink room."

"That's right, a pink room. Your bedroom, right?"

"Yeah!" She grinned. "I had a clown collection."

Simon groaned and laughed, suppressing a shudder. The clowns had always freaked him out a little. Creepy little things. No wonder he blocked the memory. "You did. They sat on your windowsill."

"My clowns. Can I see them?"

"In a moment. I want you to remember something else." He glanced out the window. "Can you picture who lives there? Who is inside?"

"Hmm." This time, her thinking face included pushed down eyebrows. "A man. And a lady."

"Yes?"

The seconds ticked by.

"Oh." Her voice became a breathy whisper. "Mom and Dad."

She leaned through the seats, grasping Simon's sleeve. Staring. Frozen. "Mom and Dad are in there."

"Yeah, they are." He shook her hand off playfully. "Well, go on, kid. Go home."

She had trouble getting the car door open—had to fumble with the automatic locks—but managed.

Sarah didn't look when crossing the street, so intent was she on the old house with the big bay windows and faded yellow curtains. Simon had to stall an oncoming Toyota just so she wouldn't get mowed down. Didn't even look like she noticed the car that had rolled to a stop a few yards from her.

She paused to brush her hands against the clematis blossoms hugging the fence post. Slowly, she walked up the sidewalk, testing each footstep, looking in every direction.

Knocking twice, she turned on the door step to look back at him and smiled, one last time, the same wide toothy smile she'd given him all those years ago. She was the same Sarah he'd lost. And she was finally found.

The pain that lanced through his heart was a different kind, sharp and fresh. He wanted to keep her just a moment longer, just enough to let it all sink in. Just one more moment of feeling like he had everything he'd thought was forever lost. That toothy grin, maybe another bout of laughter. Precious things that couldn't be tallied and couldn't be his again.

It was selfish, but he probably could have done it. Thrown up a cloaking spell and portaled the hell out of there to a fixed moment in time, where the sands in the hourglass paused mid-stream. But keeping her a moment longer would have been a greedy thing. It would have spoiled all the good that had finally been done.

Remembering his place, he swallowed hard and denied the impulse to clutch tight that bit of happiness. He had to let go. This time, he could let her go to a good place. That knowledge was the only thing he could allow himself to keep.

He waved his fingers and murmured, setting the final part of the spell. Sarah's smile faltered, confusion drifting in while she looked at him. *Do I know you?*

He let his breath leak out. Only her manufactured memories remained. Good. Slowly they'll be replaced with ones of a happy reunion.

The door opened and her mother cried out at the sight of her, her father close behind. Crying and shouting, laughing and hugging, the family, reunited at long last, disappeared into the house, the door closing behind them, a new life before them. The sounds of happy tears drifted through the open windows.

Simon watched silently, knowing there would never be such a homecoming for him.

Chiara rubbed his arm. "You did it. You brought her back. It's over."

He shook his head, a quick negation, and blew out a breath. He wasn't looking at Sarah's house. He stared beyond it at the plain house next door. "Far from it."

Tugging out a chicory stick and his lighter, he opened the car door and got out.

Chiara leaned over her seat. "What are you going to do?"

"Clean up my mess." He swung the door shut. His jaw clenched, he walked slowly past Foster's to the house next door, a plain square of a two-story home Chiara had remarked how out of place it looked when they drove past it the morning before. He crossed the lawn, steps slowing as he got halfway to the porch, his hands raised. Coming to a standstill, he lit the chicory stem and exhaled into the smoke, blowing it forward.

A barrier glinted and sparkled briefly, revealed by the smoke. He rapped on the barrier, two taps with his knuckle, and stepped back to watch. The shimmer streaked outward in all directions, hinting at a great dome that covered the property. Nodding to himself, he shoved his fingers into his pocket, pulling out a fistful of charms. He flipped through the medals and amulets until he found a crystal, a long oblong with a chiseled point at one end.

He started to chant, words that had been taught to him by *Ngangkari* from Australia's Western desert. So many years ago, he'd cloaked the remains of his childhood home within the realms of the Dreaming. It would take a lot more than chicory to pass through this ward.

He palmed the crystal shard, rotating it until the pointed end protruded from his fist, and dragged the sharp tip across his palm. Blood streaked through the split in his skin. Cupping the crimson stain until a sufficient amount had pooled, he drew a wet vertical line down the shimmering barrier, slicing it open, creating a flap.

Stepping through, Simon saw the true, undisguised ruins of his childhood home. Windows shattered, roof caving in, paint long past peeled and quite nearly gone.

Reaching into his pocket, he pulled out a smudge stick. A special one. This was no ordinary sage blend—in between the leaves were twigs of mallow, cedar shavings, lime zest and horseradish root. The smoke it would produce was sure to be a riot of smells that would most likely put him off eating for several hours, but the extra elements would boost the power of the cleansing.

Exorcism. Protection. Healing.

Love.

A weathered letter from the sheriff's office plastered the front door. If Simon looked hard, he might have been able to make out the date. He hadn't looked when he placed the property into this pocket of the Dreaming, and he had no plans to look now. Placing a hesitant hand on the wood, he pushed, just a little. The door cracked off its rotted hinges and fell open.

He ducked through the dismantled doorway into the dim shadows. A part of his spirit crumpled to see what was left. Debris covered the floors, dead leaves and ceiling tiles. The floors were splintered, shoved up in shards after the pipes had frozen and exploded. The walls were mottled with musty-smelling spots, the paint peeled. Everywhere was decay and destruction.

Nowhere was any sign of the home it once had been, so very long ago. Mom wasn't in the kitchen, following along with some cooking show chef. Sarah wasn't playing on her swing set in the backyard next door. No happy reunion here. Just the ghosts of regrets and immaturity and very, very poor judgement.

He tugged a feather out of his jacket. Time to banish those ghosts.

He vestured as deep into the parlor as he dared, kicking the trash and the rot out of the way, clearing a space. Opening a small amphora, he carefully poured the contents out in a circle around him. Salt with a kick. This circle needed to hold. He stooped and peered at the thick line. A quick inspection showed it was intact, no breaks or skips. So he hoped.

If he was wrong, at least it would be his last mistake.

He took a deep breath and held the smudge stick to the flame of his lighter, waving it to get the smolder going. The scents of sage and herb stung his nose as he turned to each of the four directions, wafting the smoke and chanting.

Creaking in the ceiling started first, groaning in the walls followed. Clatters beneath him sped his pulse. Simon closed his eyes and continued the cleansing, instinctively finding each direction, one after another. He didn't need to see the circle aglow at his feet to know it was working. He needed only to listen to the old ruins give up their grip on the past.

Boards crashed around him but he kept his eyes closed. He didn't want to see. Chanting louder, he counted the waves of the feather. One, two, three to the North. Turn on his heels. One, two, three to the East. Block out the sounds. Don't breathe in the scents. Don't watch the past come down on its knees.

Sudden sunlight danced over his eyelids, a warm ruddy glow. Count, turn, chant, sustain.

And then there was silence.

Simon finished the third wave toward the West, completing the ninth turn, and opened his eyes. He stood in the center of a square patch of soil. No rubble, no weeds, just clean scorched earth.

Almost done.

He stooped to scratch a hole between his feet and buried the remains of the sage stick, patting the soil back in place around it, before stepping out of the circle.

"Goodbye, Mom." The words came out tiny, so much smaller than the man he thought he'd become. "I have to leave. If you were here, I'd stay. But you're gone. And I have to let you go."

And then he simply walked back toward the car. The barrier let him pass without as much as a whisper across his skin.

Halfway across the street, he paused and looked over his shoulder. The ward was still in place, the plain white house that used to be a home. But the ward would fade now that he'd dissembled the power that kept it in place. The false image of the house would disappear in time for neighbors to finally remember that it had been knocked down years ago. They'd just forgotten in the excitement of Sarah Foster's return.

Memories were funny that way.

A sprinkling of tiny blue flowers popped out across the exposed lawn. Forget-me-nots. A ghost of a smile played on his lips and he glanced upwards. Whatever magic brought these bright little blossoms, it wasn't his.

He blinked, the sunlight bringing an unexpected sting to his eyes. Now. Now he could say it was done.

Epilogue

Chiara watched Simon smooth a few crumpled bills he'd found in his pockets and shook her head. "So. You barely have enough for your cigarettes, let alone a ticket back to Baltimore."

"Yeah, well." He scratched his nose. "I guess we'll have to ask Mack for a ride. That money, it was always for her. Or, at least her family. I wanted to do something for them, but never knew what. Not until you came along."

She squelched the unbidden flip her stomach made when she considered Mack and his "rides". Swallowing thickly, she persevered past the thought. "So. You do know the taste of hope, after all."

"I wouldn't call it—"

"Yes, you would. You just aren't brave enough to admit it. You're a silly superstitious man, Simon. You can't destroy a hope simply by admitting it exists."

"That's where you're wrong, love." The smile he gave her wasn't cocky, or sarcastic, or lopsided with boyish glee. It was heavy, one of sadness and resignation and acceptance. It was the smile of a man who knew exactly where he stood and wasn't proud of it. "You *can* jinx things. I should know. I made a career out of doing it."

She reached for his hand, squeezing it. "Well, you can rest that fear now. Sarah is safely home. You can't jinx a hope that has already been realized."

He turned the key and shifted into drive, pulling away. "It does feel weird to be able to breathe all the way in, you know?"

"What next, now that your demon has been banished?"

"I don't know about that. I think he'll be closer behind than ever."

"Oh. Bal." She lowered her eyes. Couldn't tell him the whole truth, could she? Couldn't say *while in Hell, I stopped by my dad's place and asked him for a favor. Balazog won't be a problem anymore.* She couldn't tell him, not without telling him how and why and who she really was. "Right. I'm sorry. I hadn't meant—"

He shushed her with a lopsided grin. "It's okay. This is my life. It's hunt and be hunted. The problems don't go away just because we set one lost girl to rights."

He stretched his arm over the back of her seat.

"Onward and upward. Clean slate. Well…" He winked. "Cleaner, anyway. It's time to see what else needs correcting. But first things first."

He rounded the corner and pulled into a convenience store parking lot. "I need a fresh pack of cigs. Back in a flash. You won't even know I'm gone."

Chiara watched him saunter in, saw him chatting with the cashier at the counter. Their eyes met through the window as he waited for his change and he smiled at her.

Suddenly, a look of sheer terror crossed his face. A split second later—

A tug on her hair, hot breath on her cheek. Someone leaned forward from the previously empty back seat.

Her breath snagged in her throat, and all she could do

was stare at Simon, his awful, telling expression, caught between one thought and the dreaded next.

The stranger wrapped her arm around Chiara's neck and chuckled, the sound dark and brittle. "Hello...Daughter."

Chiara screamed, terror flash-flooding through her.

And then, with a thunderous crash, her senses faded and she knew nothing more.

Simon watched helplessly from the checkout counter. The blinding light filled the car like a silent explosion. Cigarettes forgotten, Simon bolted outside, screaming her name.

When the light shrank, the car was empty.

She was gone.

The story will continue
in part two of The Demon Whisperer series
MURDER THE LIGHT

ABOUT THE AUTHOR

USA Today best-selling author **Ash Krafton** is a speculative fiction author from the Pennsylvania coal region. If she's not writing, it's probably because she's distracted by all the cool junk on her desk or by the stacks of books that have grown up around it.

She writes novels, short fiction, and poetry for mostly adult audiences. (She's *mostly* an adult.). Some of those novels are:

The Books of the Demimonde
(urban fantasy trilogy)

Enter the world of the Demimonde.

Look outside your window. Same old town, same streets, same people, same stories you've lived all your life. Or... are they?

Sophie Galen is an advice columnist from the suburbs of Philly. Like many sensitive women, she's done her best to create a shelter for herself in order to live in a safe, predictable world, protecting her vulnerable self: her mind, her heart, her soul.

Then he came into her life and blew the walls in.

When Marek Thurzo arrived, he brought with him all the secrets she never wanted to know: the world outside was not what she thought. There were people and creatures and powers she'd never dared to believe exist and at the very center of this humongous supernatural web was one single person.

Her. The Sophia. The one hope for redemption for the Demivampire race.

Some days, she still can't wrap her head around the whole

thing. Other days...

...she's ready to do whatever it takes to protect her demivamps, no matter the obstacle, no matter the enemy, no matter the personal cost.

While meeting her deadlines, of course. Who says a girl can't multitask while saving the world?

Bleeding Hearts, Blood Rush, and Wolf's Bane

Available in ebook, paperback, and audiobook

WORDS THAT BIND
(paranormal romance)

Social worker Tam Kerish can't keep her cool professionalism when steamy client Mr. Burns kindles a desire for more than a client-therapist relationship—so she drops him. However, they discover she's the talisman to which Burns, an immortal djinn, has been bound since the days of King Solomon...and that makes it difficult to stay away from him.

Ethical guidelines are unequivocal when it comes to personal relationships with clients. However, the djinn has a thawing effect on the usually non-emotive Tam, who begins to feel true emotion whenever he is near. Tam has to make a difficult choice: to stay on the outside, forever looking in...or to turn her back on her entire world, just for the chance to finally experience what it means to fall in love.

Ash also writes for upper YA audiences (formerly under the pen name "AJ Krafton". THE HEARTBEAT THIEF (Victorian fantasy) is a little bit Jane Austen, a little bit Edgar Allan Poe, and a whole lot of stealing heartbeats in order to stay young and beautiful forever... How far will Senza Fyne go to avoid Death?

"There was something smart, ominous, and romantic about this strange story..."

Join the Fictitious Initiative...

If you'd like an email whenever Ash has a new release, great giveaway, or special offer, you can sign up at:

http://www.subscribepage.com/b1w9p1

Thanks for reading!

Word-of-mouth is crucial for any author to succeed. If you've enjoyed reading this book, please consider leaving a brief review—just a line or two is fine, and it may help another reader decide to give this book a try.

And if you *really* enjoyed reading it, tell a friend. Friends share :)

Find more at www.Ash Krafton.com